## TESTING THE MARSHAL'S METTLE

Shanaghy touched the badge on his chest. "I have to search the place."

The big man came into the middle of the yard. "You should damn well know that tin badge ain't worth nothin' outside of town. And not very much in it."

Shanaghy smiled. "You know, Mr. Moorhouse, I like you. Now I'm going to search the premises, and if you obstruct me I'm going to throw you in jail. Now we haven't any jail, but I can shackle you hand and foot, and I'll do it. Maybe next week I'd come out to see how you're getting along, but I might forget."

He moved so quickly Moorhouse was surprised, and he stopped abruptly and half turned. Tom Shanaghy hit him.

The punch was a good one and Shanaghy could hit, but Moorhouse didn't even stagger.

"Nobody ever beat me," Moorhouse said. He caught Shanaghy with a roundhouse left that knocked him staggering and followed it up with a clubbing right that drove him to his knees. Then Moorhouse grabbed Shanaghy in his huge hands.

"Now I break your back," he said calmly.

# LOUIS L'AMOUR
# THE IRON MARSHAL

BANTAM BOOKS
TORONTO · NEW YORK · LONDON · SYDNEY

THE IRON MARSHAL

*A Bantam Book | June 1979*

| | | | |
|---|---|---|---|
| *2nd printing* ........... *June 1979* | *4th printing* ........ *August 1979* |
| *3rd printing* ........... *July 1979* | *5th printing* ...... *January 1980* |

ISBN 0–553–13781–6

*Published simultaneously in the United States and Canada*

---

*Bantam Books are published by Bantam Books, Inc. Its trade-*
*mark, consisting of the words "Bantam Books" and the por-*
*trayal of a bantam, is Registered in U.S. Patent and Trademark*
*Office and in other countries. Marca Registrada. Bantam*
*Books, Inc., 666 Fifth Avenue, New York, New York 10019.*

---

PRINTED IN THE UNITED STATES OF AMERICA

# THE IRON MARSHAL

# To My Friends, the Sales Representatives and Sales Managers from Bantam Books and Select Magazines

Smith, Bob
Smith, Larry
Snyder, Jim
Snyder, Ruth
Sobel, Shelly
Stone, Don
Sutherland, Robert
Szymik, Jim
Taylor, Harry
Thomas, Gene

Thomas, Mark
Thompson, Art
Weaver, Art
Webb, Bernalle
Williamson, Steve
Wittner, Ivan
Wofford, Fonce
Wortman, Joe
Ziccardi, John
Zurek, Mel

## SELECT MAGAZINES

Ruth Bower
Vice President
Director of Sales
Book Division

Amick, Ray
Anderson, Gary
Ankenbauer, Jim
Ayers, Robert
Barringer, Walt
Beall, Howard
Bernier, Larry
Burke, Leo
Cheslawski, Ben
Colosi, Joe
Cook, John
Eckel, Greg
Entrekin, Carson
Everett, Linda
Gudikunst, Bob
Hathaway, Ed
Harris, George
Johnson, Ronald
Karns, Ken
Karstetter, Chel
Keating, Chuck
Keegan, Bob
Kelley, Michael
Kelly, Tom
Kosar, Gary
Kreyer, Les
Lawrence, Don
Lauria, Tom
Mac Arthur, Carol
MacFayden, Doug

Martinez, Bill
McKenzie, Ken
Monkman, Diane
Murray, Bob
Newland, Chuck
Owens, George
Pesognelli, John
Poll, Gayla
Raia, Wayne
Reese, Tom
Rosefield, Doug
Rossbach, Bob
Rutledge, John
Salter, Bill
Semi, Dan
Shapiro, Mike
Siegel, Steve
Simpson, Les
Snyder, Jack
Tate, Jim
Taylor, Brian
Toth, Nick
Twigg, Bob
Vordokas, John
Williams, Sandy
Winheim, Steve
Winter, John
Woodger, Ted
Zike, Ron

*April 1, 1979*

# Chapter I

A brutal kick in the ribs jolted him from a sound sleep and he lunged to his feet. The kicker, obviously a railroad detective, stepped back and drew a gun.

"Don't try it," he advised. "Just get off."

"Now? Are you crazy? At this speed I'd get killed."

"Tough. You either jump off or you get shot off."

Shanaghy looked at the gun. "Ah, what's the use? For two-bits I'd take that away from you and make you eat it, but I'll take the jump."

He turned and swung over the edge of the open gondola, hung for an instant to gauge the speed, then dropped from the ladder. He hit the ground knees bent and rolled head over heels down the embankment, coming to his feet in a cloud of dust to hear a fading shout.

". . . an' take your dirty duds with you!"

A bundle came flying from the train and hit the ground several hundred yards further along. Then the train was past and he watched the caboose disappearing down the singing rails.

Shanaghy spat dust and swore at the disappearing train. "Ah, me lad!" he said bitterly. "There will come a time!"

He dug sand from his eyes and ears, muttering the while, and then he looked slowly around.

He stood on the bank beside the tracks in the midst of a vast and empty plain, nothing but grass, rippling in the wind. It reminded him of the sea when he crossed from Ireland.

He was thirsty, he was hungry, and he was mad all the way through. Moreover, he was bruised from the fall, adding to the bruises from what had gone before. He

stared around again. At least, they would never find
him here. He started to walk.

Suddenly he thought of the bundle thrown from the
train. Dirty duds? He had no clothing but what he wore,
and no possessions but the few things in his pocket. All
else had been abandoned when he fled.

He had been on the dodge, unable to meet his
friends for two days before he grabbed the freight train
in the yards. He had not seen his enemies but he heard
them coming. He was unarmed and the freight offered
his only chance. He took the fast-moving train on the fly
and once aboard he had fallen asleep. With daylight
he awakened but, dead tired, he dropped off to sleep
again while the train rumbled on its way. For most of
two days and nights they had traveled, so now where
was he?

He walked on until he came to the bundle. He paused,
looking down at it as it lay among the weeds and brush
near the foot of the slight embankment. A canvas haversack and a blanket-roll. He had never owned anything of
the kind.

Shanaghy slid down the embankment and picked it
up. Heavier than he expected. For a moment he considered leaving it but the blankets decided him. In a few
hours darkness would be upon him and unless he was
mistaken the nearest town was far, far away. Despite what
the railroad bull had shouted, the blankets looked re-
markably new and clean. Kneeling on the track he
opened the haversack. The first thing he found was a
slab of bacon wrapped in cheesecloth, then a small packet of coffee. "Some bindle-stiff's outfit," he told himself,
then changed his mind. There was a packet of letters,
a notebook with some loose papers tucked into it and
a map.

In the compartment behind the letters was a carefully folded suit of black broadcloth, two clean shirts,
a shirt-collar, cuff-links and a collar button. There was
a suit of underwear, just off the shelf, a razor, soap,
a shaving-brush, comb, pair of scissors and some face
lotion.

What was more important, there was a .44 pistol and
a box of ammunition. He checked the pistol. It was
loaded.

Strapping up the bag he slung the outfit over a shoulder and started on.

The hour was early, just after daylight. He plodded on, traveling, he presumed, at a rate of about two-and-a-half miles an hour. He walked beside the track to avoid the nuisance of trying to walk the irregularly spaced ties.

He saw many rabbits, a snake, and several buzzards. There was nothing else. Not a tree, not an animal, not even a large rock. Not until the middle of the afternoon when he had walked nearly twenty miles did the country begin to change. Twice the railroad crossed ravines on trestles, and finally he came to a shallow wash that seemed to rapidly narrow until it turned a bluff. He went down the embankment and followed the wash around the bluff to where it opened into a tiny basin where there were a few willows, a cottonwood or two.

On a flat place under the trees there was grass, a circle of stones for a fireplace, already blackened by use, and much broken wood. After gathering sticks and bark he got a fire started. Then he cut slices from the slab of bacon and broiled them on a stick over the fire.

He cooked and ate as he cooked, looking around. It was a snug, comfortable place. For the moment he had food, the water was good to drink and he could rest and relax. He had no idea where he was except that he was west of New York. He had never seen a map of the United States, and since arriving from Ireland when he was eleven he had never been further west than Philadelphia. He knew New York, and he had spent at least two weeks in Boston.

They would never find him here, but they'd be looking. Well, so let them look.

Nobody had ever said Tom Shanaghy was a nice man. From boyhood he had been a tough, iron-fisted bruiser, starting at six when he had helped his father in their blacksmith shop, shoeing horses, mending carts, sharpening plow-blades or whatever needed it.

His father, accepting a cash payment for joining up, had become a farrier . . . a horse-shoer . . . for the army and had gone out to British India. According to reports, he was killed there. Tom and his mother had emigrated to America, but she died on the way over and

Tom Shanaghy landed in New York alone, without friends and without money.

He had walked off the boat into trouble. A boy about his own age, standing with a group of boys, called him "a dirty Mick," and Shanaghy replied the only way he knew. He went in swinging. His first swing dropped the boy who had yelled at him, his second swing dropped a companion, and then they were all over him.

He was alone and there were seven or eight of them. He slugged, kicked, bit and gouged, fighting with all he had because he was alone. Then suddenly another boy was beside him, a boy he had seen on the ship but had not known.

They were getting the worst of it when he heard a harsh voice. "Stop it, damn y'! Let the lads up!"

The boys who had started the fight scrambled to their feet, took one look and fled.

He was a big, burly man, almost six feet but strongly made. He wore a handlebar mustache and his nose had been broken. His knuckles were scarred with old cuts.

He took the cigar from his teeth. "What's y' name, bye?"

"Shanaghy, sir. Tom Shanaghy."

"Well, you're a fighter. A good fighter. Y' can take 'em as well as hand 'em out." The man turned sharply and looked at the other boy. "And who are you, m' lad?"

"Pendleton, sir. Richard Pendleton."

"Aye. Well, you've a way with your fists, too, and and you're a friend of Shanaghy's?"

"Not exactly, sir. We came over on the same vessel, but did not meet until now. He was in a bad fight, sir, and it seemed only fair that I should have a part of it. I do not like seeing such an unequal fight."

"Nor I . . . unless it's on my side they are. You're a strong lad. But you two be off wi' you now. It's not a good place for you."

Shanaghy wiped the blood from a cut over his eye. "Sir? It's an important man y' are, as anybody with half an eye can see. Have y' no friends that might need a strong lad? It's alone I am, for my good mother died on shipboard."

The big man took the cigar from his teeth, his eyes glinting with a cynical humor. "Ah? A smart lad, an' not above a bit o' the blarney." From a pocket he took a slip of paper, and on it wrote a few words. "Here's a street an' the number. You'll be askin' for a man name of Clancy. Tell him Morrissey sent you."

"And my friend as well?"

Morrissey started to speak but Richard Pendleton interrupted. "No, thank you. No need to speak for me. I've a place to go and people who will be meeting me. Thank you."

Morrissey walked away and the two boys looked at each other. Shanaghy was strongly built with black hair and blue eyes, a sprinkling of freckles over his nose. Pendelton was wiry and had light brown hair, somewhat the taller.

"Thanks," Shanaghy said. "You're a fine fighter and you saved me a beating."

"It was Mr. Morrissey saved up both. Did you notice? They are afraid of him. He had only to speak, and they ran."

"He's a big man."

"I think he's more than that. I think he is John Morrissey, the prizefighter and gambling man."

"Never heard of him."

"My father told me of him, among others. He is . . . or was . . . the heavyweight champion at bare-knuckle fighting."

The boys had then shaken hands and parted, Shanaghy to seek his job.

It was a restaurant and saloon. There were a dozen men in the place and he asked for Clancy. "Yonder, by the door. But speak softly, he's in a foul mood."

He crossed the room to Clancy and stopped before him. "I'm Tom Shanaghy. I've come for a job."

"You've come for a job? Beat it, boy! I've no jobs and no time for ragamuffins in off the street."

"Mr. Morrissey gave me this. It is for you." Shanaghy handed him the note, and as he glanced at it the tall, thin man beside him looked over his shoulder.

"You know Morrissey?"

"I do."

"Clancy, don't argue with the lad. That's Old Smoke's fist . . . No other could write like him. You've no choice."

"All right," Clancy said irritably. "Make yourself useful." Abruptly, he walked away.

The tall man smiled. "It's all right, boy. Clancy doesn't like being told what to do, and least of all by Old Smoke. However, he'll stand by it. You've a job, then." As an afterthought, he added, "I'm his partner here . . . Henry Lochlin. You get into the kitchen and help with the dishes, clean up around. There'll be plenty to do, and don't worry about Clancy. He isn't as mean as he sounds."

That was the way of it. He washed dishes, swept floors, peeled potatoes and ran errands.

A week later Henry Lochlin stopped beside him. "You're a good lad and you're doing well. You've worked before this, I take it?"

"Aye . . . My father was a farrier, sir. We shod the horses of all the gentry, and I raced some of them."

Lochlin looked at him again. "You've ridden races?"

"Aye, on the dirt and on the turf, steeplechase as well. I rode first when I was nine, sir. That is, my first race was then. I've been up eleven times, sir."

"Good stock, those Irish horses."

"The best, sir. The very best."

"Did you win at all?"

"Three times, sir. We were in the money seven times, Mr. Lochlin."

"You're small for those big Irish horses."

"But strong, sir. I helped my father with the work. I have shod horses myself, a time or two."

Lochlin nodded. "One of these times, drop in on McCarthy. He's got a blacksmith shop down the block. He might need help."

McCarthy was a pleasant man, and a good smith. Shanaghy recognized that at once, and watched him with pleasure. His own father had been good or else they'd never have let him shoe all that racing stock, but this man was good, too.

"If a man would live he must be the best," McCarthy said, one day. "There's many a smith in New York City, and there's more than two hundred thousand horses in the town, bye. Two hundred thousand! Did you think of that? Each horse will drop twenty-five or -six pounds of manure per day, and there's a stable in near every block on Manhattan! Think of that! The day will come when they will not tolerate a stable or a kept horse in the city! You'll see!"

"But how will they get about?"

"There'll be a way. Steam cars . . . someway."

"But what of you, then?"

"Ah, lad, there be three to four thousand on Manhattan who say they shoe horses, but there's but a few to whom I'd trust a good horse." He looked sharply at Shanaghy. "Your pa was a farrier? What happened to him?"

"He went out to India with the soldiers. He was needed, they said. He turned up missing after an attack and is thought to be dead. Many were killed that time, and I am sure he was, too. With the hot weather and all, they don't let bodies lie about waiting to be identified."

"Aye, 'tis the way of war. Many go and few return, and what happens to some of them you never know." McCarthy glanced at him. "What is it you want for yourself? To be a waiter in a saloon? It isn't much, lad. Better your father's trade and to go west."

"West? Where is that?"

"Ah, lad, there's a wide land beyond us here! A far, beautiful land. They do be sayin' there's gold yonder, and silver, and all manner of things. Mostly there's land free for the taking."

"And the savages."

"Aye. They be there, but there's savages enough in the city, too." He paused, hammer in hand. "It is a rough place where you be workin', lad. There's mostly women of no account, and among the men there's thieves and worse. 'Tis no fit place for a lad."

"It is what I have, and Mr. Morrissey sees after me."

"Aye . . . when he's of a mind to, and when he's sober. I like old John, don't you forget that, but he's a rough 'un, battered his way up with two hard fists and his wits and now he walks among the swells. Some of them sneer at him behind his back, but it is behind his back. They are all afraid of him, and when election comes he can get out the votes. Why," he added grimly, "it is said that even the dead come to life and vote when he speaks, and well enough it can be true, for I've seen the names of those dead these three years, and still voting!"

Tom Shanaghy chuckled, shaking his head. "He's the canny one!"

McCarthy spat. "Aye, but a man'll get nowhere if he's dishonest. Chickens come home to roost, me bye. Ride a straight trail and y'll get farther and feel better, and have no worry about what someday will be discovered.

"Those who are dishonest will be dishonest with you, too, and when it suits them will turn on y'. Among such folks y' trust no man . . . and, particularly, no woman."

Shanaghy shrugged. Who was McCarthy to talk? He ran a blacksmith shop he did not even own. Morrissey had a saloon, a restaurant, and who knew what else? People walked wide around him and spoke to him with respect.

His mother, he reflected, had sounded just like McCarthy, but what did she know? She'd never been three miles from her own village until they went to the ship. A fine woman, a decent woman, but she did not know much about life.

He was remembering all that as he made his camp. He took his blanket-roll back under the trees in the deepest shadow. He liked being close to the fire but was a little afraid of it, too. In New York they sometimes talked of the West and the Indians and he knew they were canny at hunting. He did not wish them to come upon him in the night.

He unrolled the blankets and it was then he found the shotgun. It was in two pieces, needing merely to be put together, and there was a tube container evidently made to contain the two pieces of the shotgun. Now it was filled with shells. He put the shotgun together and loaded it.

Lying on his back, hands clasped behind his head, Tom Shanaghy listened to the rustle of the leaves and watched the fire dying. Tonight, for the first time in a long while, his thoughts kept returning to Ireland.

It had been good there. Hungry, those years after his father went away, but good years in a green and lovely land. At first his father had sent them a little, then came the news that he was missing in action.

Almost twelve years now he had stayed in New York, and that, too, had been hard . . . from the very first. Nearly every day he had a fight, and the boys he met were tough and street-wise, as schooled in fighting as he, but they lacked his natural quickness and the strength developed from the blacksmith's hammer and the hard work on the farm. He whipped them all.

All but Pegan Rice. The larger, older boy had whipped him four times. But while he was getting whipped, Tom Shanaghy was learning. Pegan had a bad habit of dropping his left after punching with it, so one time they fought Tom took the left going in and swung with his right. The punch went over the left to Pegan's chin, and the timing was right. Pegan went down hard. He got up, Tom feinted, Pegan threw the left and Tom slipped it and crossed his right to the chin again. After that he saw no more of Pegan Rice.

Shanaghy became a runner for John Morrissey, taking the word to gamblers and gambling houses, to the women on the line and to the ward heelers who did his bidding.

Yet two or three times each week he managed to work with McCarthy for an hour or two, sometimes the whole day. Despite the hard work, or perhaps because of it, he enjoyed himself. And he liked McCarthy. The old Irishman was a tough, no-nonsense sort of man, untouched by the corruption about him.

When not with McCarthy, his haunts were the saloons and dives.

Men such as Morrissey, who could swing the Irish vote, were important to Tammany Hall and, shrewdly, Morrissey had worked hard to make himself even more so. Admired for his fighting abilities, he was also a politician who found newcomers a place to live. He found them jobs, kept them out of trouble. His thugs and "shoulder-strikers," as they were called, frightened opposition voters away from the polls, protected their own voters, and occasionally stuffed ballot-boxes or engaged in all manner of trickery and deceit.

Basically, it was Morrissey's personal popularity that usually carried the day for him.

Shanaghy was thirteen years old when he glimpsed an old friend. He was coming up through the Five Points, walking the middle of the street as behooved one who knew the area, when he saw the Maid o' Killarney . . . She was hitched to a butcher's wagon.

He walked to the curb and stopped. Appearing to pay no attention, he looked the horse over carefully. The same scar on the inside of the fetlock, identical markings. It had to be.

The horse, left standing while a delivery was being made, suddenly took a step forward, stretching its nose to him. "Aye, Maid, you remember me, don't you?" He patted her a little, and when the driver came bustling from the house he commmented, "Nice horse."

"Feisty," the delivery man said testily, "too feisty."

Tom had glanced at the sign on the side of the wagon, then waved a hand and walked up the street. Once he was out of sight, he ran.

Morrissey, Tom knew, had a meeting at his gambling house at No. 8 Barclay Street, and he should be there now.

Tom entered the gambling house and saw Morrissey seated at a table with several other men, a beer and a cigar clutched in his big hands. Tom hesitated, then walked to Morrissey and spoke up.

"Sir? Mr. Morrissey?" Old Smoke did not like to be interrupted, and he turned sharply. When he saw the boy, some of the irritation left his eyes. "What is it, bye? What's wrong?"

"Sir, I must speak with you. Now, sir."

Astonished, Morrissey stared at him. In the year and a half since he had first seen Tom Shanaghy, the boy had never ventured to speak unless spoken to. He had kept out of the way, had done what he was told and kept his mouth shut.

"What is it, then?"

"Alone, sir. I must speak to you alone."

Morrissey pushed back his chair. "If you'll excuse me a moment, gentlemen?"

Taking his beer in one hand and cigar in the other, he led the way to a secluded table. He sat down and gestured for Tom to sit opposite. "Now what is it, bye? I am a busy man, as you can see."

"Sir, I've just seen the Maid o' Killarney!"

"The who? Who or what is this Maid o' Killarney?"

"A horse, sir. A racehorse. She's drawing a butcher's wagon in the Five Points."

Morrissey put the cigar in his teeth. "A racehorse drawing a butcher's wagon? She must be no good. Must have busted down."

"I don't think so, sir. She looked fit . . . only not cared for, sir. I know the mare, sir. She was uncommonly fast, and even if she's not in the best of shape she could still be bred, sir."

"All right, lad. Take your time and tell me about her . . ."

How long ago was that? Tom Shanaghy, hands clasped behind his head, looked up at the rustling leaves. Ten years? A long time back, a very long time.

Slowly and carefully he had explained to John Morrissey about the Maid. How he had been present when she was born, how he had ridden her as an exercise boy around the stables, and ridden her in her first race.

"The Maid won," he explained. "Then she won again. She won twice more with somebody else up, then the man who owned her got in debt over gambling. He lost her and she was sold to an American."

Morrissey dusted the ash from his cigar. "You're sure of the horse?"

"I am. It was my father fitted the first shoes to her. I played with her as a boy. I'd not make a mistake. And she remembered me."

"How old would she be?"

"Five . . . a bit over."

Two days later Morrissey called him in. "Tom, me bye, how would you like to drive a butcher's wagon?"

"Whatever you say."

"You've got a job, then. You'll drive the wagon and you'll check the horse. As I understand it the deliveries are over by noon. You'll take the horse to Fenway's after you've finished. Tomorrow is Saturday. Sunday morning take her out on the track and give her a light workout. Easy does it. See how she moves, if anything is wrong wi' her.

"Lochlin will be there, and he's a fine horseman. He will be watching. No trying for speed now, for she's been living poorly and will have to be taken careful. Above all, don't y' touch her with a curry-comb or anything of the kind.

"And not a word of this to anyone, y' understand? Not a word!"

Sunday morning the air had been cool with a touch of fog in the air. He led the Maid out to the track and Lochlin gave him a leg up.

"Once around. Just see how she moves, lad. Maybe we have something and maybe we don't."

When they turned into the track, the Maid remembered. Her head came up and she tugged at the bit. "Not now, baby. Take it easy . . . easy now!"

She moved into a canter and went once around the track. Lochlin was waiting for them when he pulled up near the gate.

"Moves well. Seems a little stiff, that's all."

Tom took her around again, a little faster. She was eager and wanted to run and he had to restrain her.

"How was she when you rode her?" Lochlin asked when they returned.

"She's a finisher, Mr. Lochlin. She likes to come from behind, and if she's anything like she used to be she can really run."

For a week he drove another horse, much alike in outward appearance, with the butcher's wagon. In the afternoons he worked out the Maid. She had a natural affinity for the track, loved running, and liked to win. What Morrissey had in mind he had no idea, except that he expected to make a lot of money.

"Tom," Morrissey said one day, "don't come around to Barclay Street." He lit a fresh cigar. "There's a man who comes there to gamble. Quite the sharper he thinks himself, and he has a horse. He's been doing a bit of bragging about that horse, and I've a friend wishes to take him down a bit."

It had been a week later that Tom was driving the Maid with the butcher's wagon. He had a delivery that morning that took him to Barclay Street and he had stopped to get packages of meat from the wagon when he saw Morrissey. Several men were with him and he heard one of the men say, "What? Why, that Wade Hampton horse of mine could beat either of them! Either of them, I say!"

Shanaghy heard the arrogance in the tone but did not look around, although he wished to.

"Bob," another voice said, "you've been doing a lot of talking about that Wade Hampton horse. We hear a lot but we don't see any action. I think you're just talking through your hat!"

"Like hell, I am! He's won his last six races, and he'll win the next six. If you want to put your money where your mouth is, Sweeney, just find yourself a horse!"

"Bah!" Sweeney was contemptuous. "I don't own a horse, and you know it, but I think you're full of hot air! Why, I'd bet that milk-wagon horse could beat yours!"

"What?"

The Maid, in blinders and a fly-net, stood waiting while Tom poured milk into a can, her head dropping as she snuffled at the dust along the curb.

"Don't be a fool, Sweeney!" another of the men protested. "That mare is all stove up. Anyway, an animal like that can't run. All she can do is pull a wagon."

Lochlin emerged from the gambling house. "What's that? What's going on?"

"Sweeney just offered to bet that milk-wagon horse could beat Bob Childers' Wade Hampton. He wasn't serious, of course, but—"

"The hell I wasn't!" Sweeney said angrily. "You damn right I'm serious! Bob carries on about that nag of his like it was the only horse in the world! Well, I think Bob's full of hot air!"

Lochlin shrugged. "You can't be seriously suggesting that that old nag could outrun a racehorse? You've got to be crazy, but if you're serious I'll lay twenty to one that Wade Hampton can beat him."

"Twenty to one? I'll take it!"

Sweeney hesitated. "Well now . . . See here. I don't know if—"

"Going to welsh on it, Sweeney?" Bob Childers asked. "You said I was full of hot air, what about you?"

"I'll be damned if I am! I said I'd bet and I will. Twenty to one . . . And I've got a thousand dollars says the milk-horse wins!"

"*A thousand dollars?*" Morrissey spoke for the first time. "That's serious money, Sweeney."

"I've got it and I'll bet it," Sweeney said stubbornly. "Bob, you an' Lochlin can put up or shut up."

"Think what you're doing, Sweeney. Bob has a racehorse. That old milk-wagon horse is stiff and old. Hell, if she ever could run, she can't any more. I'd say forget it."

"He made his bet," Lochlin said, "and I've accepted. I will put up my money on one condition. That we run the race tomorrow."

Lochlin turned to Childers. "Bob," he spoke softly, "this will be the easiest money we ever made. I knew Sweeney was a damn fool, but I didn't realize how *much* of a damn fool he was! This will be a cinch. I'll pick up a cool thousand for an investment of twenty thousand, and all in a matter of minutes." He paused. "How much are you betting, Bob? You can take him for plenty because

he's too bullheaded to back out, and you know Sweeney
. . . he's got it to bet."

"I don't know," Childers frowned. "I've got to think
about it."

"He's good for plenty, Sweeney is, and he's that much
of a damn fool. You'll never have a chance like this
again. I would guess he's good for twenty or thirty thousand, and I can come up with another twenty. If you can
come up with sixty thousand we can win it all. It's a cinch."

"It's a lot of money," Childers muttered.

"Of course, but it will take you a year to clear that
much . . . Hell, it would take three good years to clear
that much in your saloon. If the man's a fool, let's get
his money before somebody else does."

"Where does Morrissey stand? Is he in with us?"

Lochlin shrugged. "He's not involved, so far. You can bet
if he sees what we've got, he'll be in for a piece, but John
was never much of a gambler. He operates the places but
he doesn't gamble."

That was ten years ago or better! Shanaghy remembered the day of the race. He had been up on the Maid
and they purposely tossed dust over her, and brought her
on the track looking like the milk-wagon horse she'd
been. But Shanaghy was nervous, for it was impossible to
disguise the clean lines of her.

Wade Hampton had started fast and well and was leading by three lengths when the horses rounded the back
turn. Then Tom let the Maid go. Filled with joy at the
chance, the horse began to run. When they came under the
wire she was running easily and won by half a length.

Morrissey had cautioned him. "Lad, if you look to be
winning, don't make it by too much, understand? We can
use this horse again."

The Maid won, and Sweeney, Lochlin and Morrissey
split sixty thousand dollars among them.

Shanaghy told McCarthy about the race, and the old
blacksmith straightened up from his work. "Aye, I heard
of it, lad. And you were a part of that? You should be
ashamed. It was a swindle. All of them should be ashamed.
Ah, if their old mithers but knew of it!"

"But Mr. Lochlin lost money, too!" Shanaghy protested.

McCarthy spat. "If you believe that, you're more innocent than I believed. Did you see any of Lochlin's money?
Did anybody?"

"Gallagher was holding the bets. He said—"

"Aye, Gallagher! One of the same lot! Believe me, lad, Lochlin was the come-on, he was the pusher. Lochlin talked a good bet but he was in it up to his ears. And as for Morrissey, he was the brains of the lot—and seemed to be out of it all so he'd not be suspected. Old Smoke is a shrewd man, lad, and don't you forget it. Running for the state Senate, he is, and he'll be elected, too. You fight shy of that lot, lad, or you'll end in jail!"

Morrissey had given him five hundred dollars for tipping them off to a good thing and riding the horse. It was more money, Shanaghy reflected, than his poor pa had seen in his lifetime. With it, Shanaghy bought some new clothes and a better place to live. He put three hundred of it into a bank McCarthy suggested.

He had ridden the Maid in three more races before he grew too heavy for riding. By the time he was sixteen he was five feet nine inches, as tall as he was ever to be, and he weighed an easy hundred and sixty but looked lighter. Sometimes he sparred with Old Smoke himself, but the iron-fisted Irishman was rough, with both height and reach on Shanaghy, who learned to ride and slip punches, to bob and weave and move in and away.

Although a middleweight in size, he had the shoulders and punching power of a heavyweight, and several times they rang him in on unsuspecting country fighters larger than he.

Of Bob Childers or his family he saw nothing more until several months later when, emerging from the Five Points, he came upon a man who looked like Bob Childers' son standing on a corner with two other men.

"There's one of them now," one of the men said, pointing at Tom. "He rode the horse."

The burly young man who resembled Childers called out to him. "You! Come here!"

Shanaghy paused. He knew he should keep going, but something in the young man's tone irritated him. "You want to see me," he said, "come to where I am."

"I'll come, an' be damned to y'!"

Shanaghy was convinced this was Bob Childers' son. He was a powerful young man, yet too heavy. Shanaghy stood waiting, watching the other two men as well. When the young man was almost to him he saw the others start, and he knew it would be not the one but all three he must fight. The first one stepped up on the curb. "You're one o' that pack o' thieves," he said, "and I'm going to teach you!"

"Your pa bought himself a horse race and he lost," Shanaghy said to the young man. "That's all. He asked for it with his loud mouth."

"Loud mouth, is it?" The young man lifted a ponderous fist threateningly. "I'll teach . . ."

If you are going to fight, Shanaghy had learned long since, don't waste time talking. As young Childers stepped up on the curb, Shanaghy went quickly to meet him. He smashed a left to Childers' mouth; then swung a right into his belly. The punch caught Childers moving in and was totally unexpected. A strong young man, Childers knew little of fighting and always had much to say before he swung a fist. This time he never said it. His wind left him with an *oof* and he staggered and fell back into a sitting position. Shanaghy wheeled and dove into the space between two buildings, ran their length and, turning sharply, mounted the stairs to the upper story.

This was an area he knew well. Emerging on the rooftop, he ran along the roofs, jumping the walls that divided one from the other. Soon he was blocks away. Coming down from the final rooftop, he went to his room.

A few days later he saw John Morrissey. "Aye," John said, "we bought ourselves a packet, lad. Bob's a beefhead himself, but some of the money was from his brother, Eben, and that's another thing. Eben Childers is uncommon shrewd, and a mean, mean man. The one you hit was not Bob's son but Eben's, so you've made an enemy. Be on your guard, lad, for they'll stop at nothing until you're killed or maimed. He believed that big son of his was unbeatable and you felled him with a blow."

Shanaghy shrugged it off. So he had made an enemy . . . Well, he had made enemies before this one. Yet it was little he knew of Eben Childers then, and he cared even less, for he had been fighting for half his life and knew nothing else.

"He's a hater, lad, and don't forget it. He lost money, but worse than that he was made to appear a fool, and he's a proud, proud man."

The word got around that Childers was recruiting men for an all-out war with Morrissey, and Childers had influence where it mattered. Unexpectedly, Morrissey found doors closed to him that had always been open, but Shanaghy knew little beyond the casual barroom gossip that he picked up.

Then, one night, as he was coming up the Bowery, he was set upon by a gang of thugs who emerged suddenly from a doorway. "Break his legs!" somebody shouted. "Break his legs and his fingers!"

Again they reckoned without his knowledge of the area, for Tom lunged suddenly, meeting them as they came, and his iron-hard fist clipped the nearest man. The man fell. Leaping past him Shanaghy darted up a stair with the men hot after him. As he topped the flight, he turned. Then grasping a rail in either hand, he swung both feet up and kicked out hard. The boot heels caught the nearest man in the face and he toppled, knocking those behind him backward down the stairs. Again Shanaghy escaped over the roofs.

When he came warily down from the roofs, a few doors from his room, he held himself still in the doorway while he looked carefully around. He was hot and tired. He wanted nothing so much as to climb the stairs to his own room and fall on the bed, yet he was wary.

He had started to leave the doorway where he was hidden when he caught a flicker of movement in the shadows up the street. Was it a harmless drunk sleeping it off in a doorway? Or some of Childers' men waiting for him?

No use taking the chance. He went back to the roofs. Almost a block further along, he descended to McCarthy's blacksmith shop. The place was locked and silent, so he crawled into a wagon, pulled a spare canvas wagon-sheet over him and went to sleep.

Shanaghy awakened to the clang of McCarthy's hammer. He sat up, rubbing his eyes. The sides of the wagon were high, and he could not see the wagon-yard or the doorway to the shop. He stood up, grasped the side of the wagon and swung himself over. As his feet hit the ground he heard a rush of feet behind him. Instantly he ducked under the wagon and came up on the other side.

A man started under the wagon after him, and Shanaghy kicked him in the head, then turned to face the two who had come around the end of the wagon.

One of them yelled, "There he is! *Get him!*"

Suddenly McCarthy was in the door of his shop, holding a hammer. "One at a time!" he shouted. "Or I'll bust some skulls!"

The man who came at him was a beefy shoulder-striker from Childers' crew. It was a big, broad man with blond hair and a florid face who rushed at Shanaghy. The moment he put up his two ham-like fists, Shanaghy knew he might be good in a rough-and-tumble, but he was no boxer. The man came in, looping a wide right for Shanaghy's chin, and Shanaghy crouched and came in whipping two underhanded punches into the bigger man's belly.

The two punches were perfectly timed. A right to the belly, a left to the same place and then an overhand cross to the chin, and the man went down. He tried to get up but slumped back down into the dirt.

Turning sharply, Shanaghy hit the other man before he expected it, knocking every bit of wind out of him. As the man doubled up, Shanaghy gave him a knee in the face.

The first one was crawling out from under the wagon, a streak of blood on his face. He held up a hand. "No! No! I quit!"

"Be off with you, then," Shanaghy said, "but don't come looking for me again."

When they had gone, Shanaghy went into the blacksmith shop and pumped a bucketful of water from the well. He stripped to the waist and bathed his chest and shoulders, then dampened his hair and combed it out.

"Well," McCarthy said dryly, "it seems you can fight a little, and it seems you must. They be upon you, lad."

"Aye. I slipped them last night when they lay waiting at my house." Tom dried his hands. "I think I must take it to them a bit."

"Be careful, lad. There's a mean man there, that Eben Childers. He's a hard one, and cold. And his boys . . . You met the least of them in Bob. There's others . . . worse."

McCarthy watched Tom put on his shirt. "Lad, why don't you go west? There's a deal of land out there, and a chance for a young man."

"Land? I'm no farmer, Mac."

"Aye, that you aren't. But what are you, then? A shoulder-striker for Morrissey? A street thug? A bum?

Look at yourself, lad, and look well. Just exactly what are you? A fine broth of a lad who is nothing . . . Nothing, do y' hear me? And if you stay here hanging about with thugs, cardsharps and the like, you'll be nothing more until they pick you from the gutter some day."

Shanaghy glared at him. "Have a care, old man."

"Old man, is it? Well, *I've* grown old . . . Will you ever? You'll end with a broken skull some night and they'll have you off to bury in potter's field.

"What are you that any bum along the street is not? There's ten thousand like you in Five Points and they'll all die and come to nothing. You're young, and the land is wide. Why stay here where there's few chances? Why not go west? You could study law, study anything, make a man of yourself."

"I'm not a man?" Tom doubled his arm. "Look at that. Eighteen inches of biceps. Who can say I'm not a man?"

"Aye, you're strong, but what else are you? Have you got the brains God gave you? Or a head fit only for butting, like a billy goat?

"If a man is to be something, if he is to be a man, he's got to be more than muscle. He's got to do something wi' himself. Get an honest trade, a bit of land, a house of your own, if it is only of sod. Here your friends pat you on the back and let you buy them drinks or whatever, but when you get old and fat and sloppy they'll drop you for others. Men like you are born to be used and tossed aside . . . *if* you let it happen."

"What are you? A priest? When did you start preaching, Mac?"

"It's a bit of warning, that's all. You're a fine lad, so why become what you're becoming? There's a bigger, wider world than any slum, and a man only stays there because he hasn't the guts to get out. There's other people, other places, and you can make new friends, worthwhile friends."

Shanaghy stared at McCarthy with disgust. He picked up his coat and slung it over his shoulder. "Thanks for keepin' them off me," he said, and walked away into the sunlight.

He strode down the street, heading for Morrissey's nearest saloon . . . the Gem. Talking to himself as he

walked along, he growled angry retorts at the distant Mc-
Carthy, saying all the things he had not said. But suddenly
they began to sound very hollow and empty.

What was he, after all? He'd ridden a few races but he
was too heavy for that now. He'd won a few fights in the
ring, but he'd no desire to make a profession of that. He
was at the beck and call of Morrissey and Lochlin, who
were important men, in their way. But what was he, himself?

He shook himself irritably. It was not a subject on
which he cared to dwell. McCarthy . . . well, what did
he know? Who was he to talk?

Yet even as Tom thought this, his good sense told him
that McCarthy wasn't worried about anybody laying for
him when he came home of a night, and he was sleeping
sound. Nor was he beholden to anybody for the money he
made. He did his job, he did it well, and he took his pay
and went home.

Now Shanaghy remembered that time all too well. He
had stopped on a street corner, thinking about it. He was
no farmer, he'd considered, but still there were towns out
west. And if he went to one of them, knowing what he
knew, he could become a big man, as big as Morrissey or
bigger.

He had fiddled around with the idea and decided he
liked it. What was that place out west? San Francisco?
He'd heard of it . . . There was gold out there, they said.

Maybe . . . he'd give it some thought.

Two days later he approached Morrissey. "Mr. Morrissey? Have you got some kind of a job for me? A permanent job?"

Morrissey rolled the cigar in his teeth, then spat into
the spittoon. "That I have, lad." He paused. "Did you
ever do any shooting?"

"Shooting? With a gun?" Shanaghy shook his head.
"No, I haven't."

"You can learn. I've got a shooting gallery. Man who
handled it for me turned into a drunk. You learn to shoot,
you get one-fifth of the take." He paused. "You try knocking down on me, bye, an' I'll have your hide off."

"I never stole anything from anybody," Shanaghy protested.

"That I know, bye. That I know. I've had my eye on

you, bye. Honest men are hard to find. Not many of them amongst my lot."

Morrissey took a slip of paper from his pocket. "Take this. You go along down to this address and give them this. I'll send a man along who will teach you to shoot. Practice all you like, and when you're good enough we'll let you win some money for us, shooting with customers."

The shooting gallery was on the Bowery amid dozens of other such establishments, pawnbrokers' shops, third-class hotels, dance houses, saloons, cheap clothing stores. Up near Prince Street was Tony Pastor's Opera House, and further down the street the Old Bowery Theater. In between was all manner of vice, trickery, and swindling, a scattering of beggars and pickpockets alert for the unwary.

At five cents a shot, there were prizes to be won—twenty dollars to anyone who could hit a bull's-eye three times in succession, and knives to be given to anyone who could hit a bull's-eye once. There was a trumpeter who, if struck in the heart, gave vent to a frightening blast on his trumpet.

Shanaghy liked the noise and confusion. Many of the sharpers he knew by sight or by name, and the same with the girls who paraded themselves along the street.

On the third morning an old man walked up to the shooting gallery. He was a lean, wiry old man with white hair and cool gray eyes. "How much for a shot?"

"Five cents . . . Twenty dollars if you hit the bull's-eye three times."

The old man smiled. "And how many times can I win the twenty?"

Shanaghy started to say, "As many times as you . . ." Suddenly he hesitated, warned by the amused look in the old man's eyes. "Once," he said. "If you hit it three times."

"Down the street," the old man said, "they let me win three times."

"Nine bull's-eyes?" Shanaghy grinned. "You're puttin' me on."

The old man took up a pistol and placed three five-cent pieces on the counter. "I'm good for business, young fellow." He placed another fifteen cents on the counter. "Six shots in here?" he asked mildly, and before he finished the words he fired. His first shot hit the trumpeter who let go with a piercing blast. People stopped and stared. Instantly, he fired again, another blast.

"Now," he said, "I'll win my breakfast money."

Without even seeming to look or to care, he fired three bullets dead center into the main target. "There . . . I'll take your twenty."

Shanaghy paid it out while people crowded around. "You got easy targets, boy. Never picked up an easier twenty in my life!" He half turned toward those gathered around. "I don't see how he can afford to operate. That's the easiest twenty I ever picked up!"

The man turned away, winking at Shanaghy. "I'll be back, son, when I need more money."

Men crowded to the counter, eager for a chance. For over an hour he was busy loading guns and handing them to customers. Once the trumpet sounded and a street-boy won a knife. It was good business, but Shanaghy kept thinking back to the old man . . . He had never seen anybody shoot like that, without even seeming to aim. The man just glanced at the target and fired . . . It was uncanny.

On the third day the same man returned and walked up to the counter, when there was nobody around. "Howdy, son. I'm short of cash."

Shanaghy, who found himself liking the old man, said, "I expected you sooner."

"You did, did you? Well, son, it don't pay to kill the goose. All I want's a livin', an' you fellows can give it to me. Costs me only twenty, thirty dollars a week to live well enough to suit me, and I can pick up that much at one stop. There's fourteen shootin' galleries along the Bowery, an' I call on each of you ever' two weeks. This time I needed some extry."

He paused. "Down the street I don't even have to take up a gun. They know I can do it, so they just pay me."

"Not me," Shanaghy grinned at him. "I like to see you shoot. I never knew anybody could shoot like that."

"Where I come from, son, you'd better be able to shoot."

"How come you're back here? Too much for you out there?"

The man's eyes chilled. "Ain't too much for me anywhere, son. I got me a sister back here. I come to visit, but there ain't nothing I can do back here but shoot. I punch cows some, yonder. And I was a Texas Ranger for a spell—have to make a livin' somehow. Then I found these here shootin' galleries. I don't want to make it hard for any of you, so I sort of scatter myself around."

"Come here whenever you're of a mind to," Tom said. "You're good for business, and I like to see you shoot. I'd give a-plenty to shoot like that."

"A body needs a mite of teachin' and a whole lot of practice. You got to get the feel for it first."

The old man put both hands on the counter. "This here is an easy livin' for me. My pa used to give me four or five ca'tridges an' I was expected to bring back some game for each loading, else he'd tan my hide for being wasteful. When it's like that, you get so's you don't waste much lead. You don't shoot until you're sure of your target and you make sure you don't miss.

"It was like that for most youngsters growin' up along the frontier. Their pa's were generally busy with farm work or whatever, so if they ate it was the meat the boys shot . . . or sometimes the girls. We had a neighbor girl could outshoot me with a rifle, but the pistol was too heavy for her."

"You didn't ever miss?"

"Oh, sure! There for awhile I got my hide tanned right often."

"You never miss here."

"At this distance? How could I? A man gets to know his gun. Each one is somewhat different, some shootin' high and to the right, some low an' left. You got to estimate and allow.

"But a man who knows guns, he wants the best, so he just naturally swaps and buys until he gets what he wants. There's more straight-shootin' guns than there are men to shoot 'em, although some of those gents out west can really shoot.

"A good many western guns been worked over. I mean, most western men doctor their guns to fit their hands better, or to shoot better, or to ease the trigger-pull . . . although 'pull' is the wrong word. No man who knows how to shoot ever pulls a trigger. He squeezes her off gentle, like you'd squeeze a girl's hand. Otherwise, you pull off target. More missin' is done right in the trigger-squeeze than anywhere else."

"I hear those redskins can't shoot worth a damn."

"Don't you believe it! Some shoot as good as any white man. And they're almighty sly about it. They don't see no sense in setting themselves up as targets, so they just pop you off from behind any rock or tree."

That was the summer when Shanaghy learned how to shoot.

# Chapter II

Shanaghy awakened in the cool hour of dawn. For a moment he lay still, trying to remember where he was and how he came to be there. He recalled being kicked off the open gondola, then went back to his thoughts about New York.

John Morrissey had gone to upstate New York on some political business, and Shanaghy, now promoted to a position as one of Morrissey's lieutenants, had dropped around to the Gem to check receipts. According to plan he had met Lochlin there. They had barely seated themselves at the table when Cogan, a bartender, stuck his head in the door.

"Mr. Shanaghy, sir? There's some men comin' in that look like trouble."

Leaving Lochlin at the table, Shanaghy stepped over to the door. He glanced quickly around. There were four men at the bar, all standing together, and there were others scattered about the room. They all had beers, but there was something about them . . .

The place was crowded, but somehow the men Cogan had mentioned stood out, and one of them . . . Shanaghy turned sharply. "Lochlin! Look out! It's Childers' men!"

He stepped quickly out into the saloon and pulled the door shut behind him. He had started around the bar when one of the newcomers deliberately knocked the beer from the hand of a bricklayer who stood beside him. The bricklayer turned to protest and the man hit him. Then they started to break the place up.

Shanaghy ducked a blow and drove a fist into the middle of the nearest man, and kicked another on the kneecap. The door crashed open and he saw a dozen men coming in, all armed with pick-handles and other clubs.

Too many! "Cogan! Murphy! *Run!*"

Shanaghy spun a table in the path of the advancing men, and when several fell he crowned them with a chair. Ducking around the bar, he armed himself with bottles which he threw with unerring aim.

Another man went down, screaming. A bottle missed Shanaghy by inches and he ducked through the door to find Lochlin. The man was gone. He had scooped up the money he was to count and scrambled out the back door.

Slamming the door into place, Cogan, who had joined him, dropped a bar across it and they ran for the alley. There were too many to fight, too many altogether.

They had almost reached the back door when there was a shot and Lochlin staggered in, bleeding.

"Upstairs!" Shanaghy told them quickly. "Over the roofs!"

He stopped and lifted Lochlin bodily from the floor, holding him in place with one arm while he scooped up the moneybag with the other. He ran up the steps, blessing his good luck for all the years at the blacksmith's anvil, and then they came out on the roof, barring the trap behind them.

The sky was covered with low clouds, and it was beginning to rain.

Murphy, another aide of Morrissey's, had joined them. "There's a rig at Kendall's," he gasped.

Suddenly, from behind a parapet of a roof, a group of men raised themselves up. Shanaghy's glance counted six. He turned. As many more were coming across the roofs behind them.

"This time," somebody yelled, "ye'll not get away!"

Shanaghy dropped the moneybag and drew a snub-nosed pistol from a waist-band holster. "I'm givin' y' fair warnin'," he said, "git to runnin' or somebody dies!"

"Hah!" a big roughneck shouted, lifting a club in one hand and a half-brick in the other, ready to throw. "Y'll not git away this . . . !"

Men had been killed with sticks and stones for millions of years before a firearm was invented, and Tom Shanaghy did not hesitate. He had been well taught, and during the four years he had operated the shooting gallery he had practiced daily.

He palmed the gun and he fired even as the big man spoke. The gun was a .44 and Shanaghy fired three times.

The big man cried out and staggered. Another fell, and then they were all running.

Somehow Shanaghy and his men got to Kendall's, got into the rig and fled. Cogan was holding Lochlin while Shanaghy drove, and never would he forget that wild night drive through the dark, rain-whipped streets.

Where should they go? Shanaghy wondered. His own place was known and would not be safe. Lochlin's bachelor quarters would be unsafe, too. Yet there was a hiding place, a place Morrissey kept off Broadway. He drove there.

There was a floor safe in Morrissey's bedroom and that was where Tom took the money. He withheld a handful of bills, made a hasty estimate and dropped a note into the safe with the remainder of the money.

> *Giving Cogan and Murphy each $100 running money. They will hide out in Boston . . . you know where. I am taking $500 and leaving $500 with Lochlin. He's hurt bad but I'll get Florrie in to take care of him. Watch yourself.*
>
>                                       *Shanaghy*

He gave money to each of the men and told Cogan to get word to Florrie to come and care for Lochlin. Then he reloaded his pistol and went to Morrissey's desk for another . . . There were two there and he took one.

He got Lochlin on the bed and bound up his wound as best he could. He'd been shot in the side and was unconscious, his clothing soaked with blood.

Florrie came to the door and he let her in, giving her Lochlin's money. "Tell nobody he's here and keep out of sight. I don't think you're known to them anyway."

"What will you do?"

"First, I've got to get that horse out of sight and into a stable. If they see it they'll trace Lochlin to this place. I'll think of myself after."

He went out through the kitchen window and down the back stairs. All was dark and silent. Thunder rumbled in the distance and there was occasional lightning. When he came out of the alley, the horse was standing there, head hanging. Shanaghy looked carefully around, then crossed the walk and got into the rig, turning the horse down the street. The top and sides kept most of the rain off. He dried his right hand and felt for his guns.

He had killed a man up there . . . perhaps two. But they were coming for him and would have killed him. His quick shooting had saved many other lives . . . probably.

He drove down the dark streets.

John Morrissey was a man who had lived with trouble, and so he was constantly aware of its proximity. Wisely, he had prepared hideouts where he could hole up until softer winds blew, and stables where horses could be found. It was to one of these Shanaghy now drove.

All was dark and silent. There were two horses in the stable and several empty stalls. Shanaghy led his horse inside, dried him off and put oats in the bin. The rig he put into a carriage house out of sight and then he went to the house hard by. Over a cup of hot coffee he considered the situation.

Eben Childers had planned well. Obviously they had known that John Morrissey was out of town. The place on Barclay Street had probably been hit as well, and Childers' men would be on all the streets. It was no time to be out and about.

Morrissey would know of what had happened within a matter of hours, but Shanaghy, knowing his man, doubted that John would make any move until the force of Childers' drive was spent. Knowing such men as Childers used, Shanaghy knew that within hours, when victory seemed complete, they would begin to drink. Some would simply turn in to rest, others would scatter to find their doxies or whatever. And that would be the time to strike.

Sitting alone in the empty house with a coal-oil lamp on the table beside him, Tom Shanaghy plotted the strategy of the days to come. He would have to get in touch with Boynton and Finlayson, and they would gather the boys for him so they could be ready to strike back.

He paced the floor, muttering to himself, trying to plan the counterattack as John would plan it, trying to foresee all that must be done.

First, he must get word to Morrissey. Then, when Boynton and Finlayson had gathered the gang together, they would choose their targets and strike.

Finally, weary with planning, he went to sleep. He awakened in the light of a chill, rainy dawn and dressed.

He checked his guns and then went down to the street. There was nobody around but he had not expected to see any people. This was a quiet neighborhood and it was Sunday.

Boynton would be in the Five Points. Shanaghy went through the streets until he reached Broadway and there he hired a hack. When he mentioned the Five Points the driver refused flatly. "No, sir, I'll not be goin' yonder. Not for any man. They'd steal the fillin's from your teeth, yonder. I'll take you within a street or two, that's all!"

No argument would suffice, and Shanaghy didn't blame him.

He found Boynton sleeping off a drunk and shook him awake. Shanaghy made coffee and forced a cup on the reluctant giant. Slowly, word by word, he filled Boynton in on all that had happened. "You're to get twenty good men . . . tough men."

He went ahead carefully with the planning. They would gather in three positions, then strike fast and hard.

John Morrissey had made enemies, and Childers had tied in with some of them. Mostly they were former followers of Butcher Bill Poole, the only man who ever bested Morrissey in a rough-and-tumble fight. Sometime later, Poole had been shot and killed by Lew Baker. That was in 1855, and the funeral procession for Poole had been the largest in the city until that time.

Several hundred policemen had led the procession, followed by 2,000 members of the Poole Association, a political faction. That was followed by nearly 4,000 of the Order of United Americans, and hose-and-engine companies from New York, Boston and Baltimore, as well as Philadelphia. As a special honor guard were two companies of militia named for Poole, the Poole Guards and the Poole Light Guards.

When the rites were completed, the various sections broke up, but the Guards and the Light Guards stayed together. It was evening before they reached Broadway and Canal Street, where a building was undergoing demolition. There, unknown to the Poole men, a number of the Morrissey faction had concealed themselves. The Original Hounds and a crowd of the Morrissey shoulderstrikers waited until the Poole men came within easy range, and then they cut loose with a shower of bricks and stones. Several Poole men went down, but they were the better-armed and charged the Morrissey faction with fixed bayonets.

Scattering, the Morrissey men took to the alleys and roofs. Yet all of them were not to escape, for later that night the Poole men attacked the engine-house where some of the Original Hounds were holed up, destroying the place and putting them to flight.

Despite the victory, the Poole forces were never again to wield their former power. Some of them, filled with hatred for Morrissey, had joined Childers.

Although Morrissey still maintained an interest in the old Gem Saloon, he no longer owned it. After operating other gambling houses, he had confined his interests to places on Barclay and Ann Street.

From Boynton's place, Shanaghy had gone on to find Finlayson. A thin, wiry man, he stared at Shanaghy and shook his head. "John's been beaten this time," he said, "beaten! They waited until he was out of town and then they moved. They've too much power."

"You believe that an' you'll believe anything," Shanaghy said. "Old Smoke has power where they've got none, an' Tammany will help him . . . if he needs it. But if we move fast—"

"Time ain't right," Finlayson objected. "They've got it all goin' their way. If John was only here . . ."

"You won't help?"

"Time ain't right," Finlayson shook his head. "You'll get yourself killed. I—"

"Forget it." Shanaghy could see that the man was frightened, his confidence shattered. "We'll do it without you."

He left on the run. He moved fast. He found O'Brien and then Larry Aiken and Linn. They were ready to move and glad somebody was doing something.

"At ten," Shanaghy told Aiken. "Don't wait for me, just move. By that time most of them will be drunk or sleeping it off."

Seated over a table he showed them on a sheet of paper how each move would be made, and when. Little did he guess that he would never be there to take part. Yet Larry Aiken was a good man, a tough man.

He remembered the night well. After leaving Aiken, he

had come out on the street and started for a livery stable. He needed a rig now. There was a place up the island where he could get some guns. Unless he missed his guess, all of Childers' men would be armed.

He hired a rig. As he was hooking the trace chains, the hostler whispered to him. "Bye, I'm a friend of McCarthy's, so watch your step! Eben's got five hundred dollars for the man who brings you in alive—to him."

The hostler paused, looking around warily. "They're after you, bye. He aims to cripple you and blind you. He's said as much."

"I'll be careful," Shanaghy said. He stepped into the rig and gathered the reins. "Open the door, then. And thanks. I'll not forget, nor will Morrissey."

He drove into the street and turned uptown. No hurry, now, he told himself. Take it easy. *Five hundred?* That was enough to turn all of the Five Points after him, and many another besides. Who could he trust?

He left Delancey Street behind him and felt better. He drove on, holding the speed down so not to attract attention. He put his hand on his gun. It was there. He felt for the other . . . it was gone! Dropped from his pocket, probably, while he hitched up the horse. He swore softly, bitterly.

Well, now. If he could get to that man on Twenty-fourth Street, he'd have guns a-plenty.

Almost an hour later, after driving around the block and seeing no one, he pulled up in an alley and stepped down. Suddenly, he was uneasy. He knew about this source of weapons, so might not Childers as well?

It was dark and silent, with only the rain whispering on the street. He put a hand on the horse's shoulder. "You wait, boy. I'll be back."

Yet he did not move. The bricks of the street pavement glistened wetly. He saw the dark maw of an alley opening toward the north, and beyond it a row of houses, each with steps and iron railings. He felt for the gun again, still irritated with himself. When had he ever trusted to a gun? Yet if there were too many of them, he must.

He studied the house where he must go. A faint light showed from under the shutters. What was the man's name?

Schneider . . . He stepped around the horse and went

quickly up the steps. There were eight steps and an iron railing on either side. Under the steps there were other steps leading down.

He lifted the knocker and rapped, not too loud. There was a sudden movement within. A chill went up his spine. Was that a movement behind him? He turned sharply . . . nothing.

Within there was a rustle of movement, and then a voice through the door. "Who is it?"

"Shanaghy," he said.

A chain rattled and the door opened . . . not a crack, but suddenly thrown wide.

There were three men! They had him then . . . No, by the . . . !

Behind him there was a scurry of feet, and Shanaghy did the unexpected. Instead of trying to turn, of trying to escape, he went at them.

He was shorter than any one of the three, but he was stronger. He went into them with a lunge, and he swung a fist at the nearest. He had hit for the man on the right, knocking him into the way of the others. Then he had the gun out and he fired.

There was a muffled blast and the hit man screamed. Turning sharply he fired into the crowd suddenly closing in behind him, then darted down the hall. He smashed open the first door he came to, saw a frightened blonde woman catch up a blanket and hold it before her, and then he was past her and throwing a chair through a window. He went out, hung for an instant, then leaped across the areaway and crashed through the glass of the window opposite.

The room was empty. He ran through it, tried to gauge the best way to go, then ran down a hall. Behind him, somebody yelled and a door slammed open. "Stop, thief!" a woman shouted.

He went up the steps three at a time, turned at the landing and ran on up. At the end of the hall he saw a gap, then a slate roof opposite him. It was wet and slippery. Behind him he heard screams and curses. He stepped to the window-ledge and leaped, catching the edge of the gutter with his hands. It broke loose at one end and he clung to the metal as it swung him toward the ground. He dropped the final ten feet and ran through a gap between the buildings.

After running down an alley, he ducked across a street, up another alley then along a street toward the north. He paused there once, to listen. They were coming, all right. They were scattering now.

Think . . . he must think.

The railroad yards, with all those cars standing, it would be dark there. He ran.

With all his hard work, he was in good shape, in better shape probably than any of his pursuers, unless some of Childers' foot-racers were among them. Foot-racing was a popular sport, and most gamblers had one or two on the payroll.

He ducked down another alley and turned into a street lined with trees. He paused, then walked on, catching his wind. He felt for the gun.

It was gone . . .

It must have fallen from his pocket back in an alley somewhere. He hoped they had not found it, that they wouldn't know he was unarmed.

Somebody crossed the street behind him and he heard a shout. He ducked into an alleyway . . . blind!

He turned back and went up the street, but they were closer now. They were spreading out, coming at him. Ahead of him there was a low fence, and he smelled wet cinders and coal smoke. Then he saw the cars. Over there was an engine, puffing thoughtfully as it waited. He dropped a hand to the fence rail and vaulted it easily, then slid down a bank and lost himself in the darkness.

A train whistled and he heard the *chug-chug* of a starting engine. Somebody fired a shot and it ricocheted over a car ahead of him.

He ducked under a row of standing cars and saw some moving cars ahead of him. He ran, caught the ladder-rung and swung himself up and over into an empty gondola.

The train gathered speed.

Behind him there were shouts and yells. They were searching. A shot . . . not aimed toward him, apparently. Gasping, he dropped to a sitting position against the side of the car.

God, was he tired!

The train whistled and he looked up to see roofs going by. It was raining harder now.

# Chapter III

When Shanaghy awakened again he lay for some time, just thinking. There was no sound but the trickling of water from the small creek and the chirping of birds. Somewhere the birds were singing an endless variety of songs. He did not know much about birds.

After awhile he sat up and looked around. He wrapped his arms around his knees and rested his chin on his arms. He had never known a morning so still . . . Yes, he had —when he was a boy in Ireland and walked to the upper pasture to bring the horses down. It had been quiet in Ireland, too.

He got up, went to the stream. After taking off his shirt, he bathed his face, head and shoulders in the cold water. It felt good. Then he rolled up his blankets. Finding a few coals left in the fire, he rekindled it and broiled some bacon.

Then he examined the guns. The pistol was a good one, brand-new, apparently. Whose outfit did he have, anyway? He belted on the gun, tried it for balance and feel. It felt good.

He had to get back to New York. That meant returning to the railroad and finding a town or a water-tank. Some place where a train might stop. He had to get back, Morrissey would need him.

Shanaghy walked back to his blanket-roll, but instead of picking it up he sat down again. Damn, it felt good! Just the stillness, the peace. After the hectic life he had been living . . .

He knew the sound of horses' hoofs when he heard them, and he heard them now. For a moment he remained where he was, just listening. Then he got up, moved the blanket-roll out of sight near a tree and leaned the shotgun against the tree. The coat he wore effectively concealed the pistol.

Shanaghy walked down to the ashes of the fire. Now maybe he could find out where he was and how far away was the nearest town.

There were four of them and they came down the slope toward the stream, riding together. One man, on a gray horse, trailed a little behind.

"Hey!" He heard one of them speak. "Somebody's . . ."

They rode through the stream and pulled up about twenty feet away from him.

"Look," one of them said, "it's a pilgrim!"

"How are you?" Shanaghy said. "I wonder if . . ."

"It's an Irish pilgrim," another said. "What d' you know about that?"

Three of them were about his own age, one of them probably younger. The fourth was a lean, wiry old man with a battered, narrow-brimmed hat and an old gray coat and patched, homespun pants. This man had his hands behind him.

Shanaghy squatted on his heels, stirring the ashes and adding a few sticks. "Headin' for town," he said casually. "How far is it?"

Some of the sticks caught a small fire.

The heavier-set of the riders took a coil of rope from his saddle and shook out a loop. He moved toward a large cottonwood. "How about here?" he suggested.

"Wait a minute," another said. "What about *him*?"

A man in a white buckskin vest had looked on but not yet spoken. He had sat, staring at Shanaghy. Then slowly he smiled. "We can always make it two," he said.

The heavy-set one looked startled. "But we don't even *know* him. He ain't done any harm."

"How do we know? He looks to me like a sinful man." He turned his full attention to Shanaghy. "Where's your horse?"

"I don't have one." Shanaghy was wary. He was in trouble but he did not know how much, nor had he quite understood what they were talking about. "I dropped off a train."

"Out here? You must be crazy! It's forty miles to the nearest town."

"I can walk."

*"Walk?* Now I know you're crazy."

The man in the white vest spoke again. "He shouldn't be here. He's in the wrong place at the wrong time."

Shanaghy was growing irritated. "This looks like a good place to me," he said. "I like it."

"You hear that?" White Vest said. "He says he likes it."

There was a moment of silence, then the man on the horse with his hands behind him said, "I always knew you were rotten, Drako."

"Bass?" Drako glanced at the man with the coiled rope. "Take him."

Shanaghy had never seen anybody rope steers, but he had heard stories from his old friend who taught him to shoot. He saw the rope go up, saw the loop shoot at him and as the horse gathered itself to leap he threw himself toward a tree. The trunk was no more than six feet from him and he was quick. For Shanaghy, to think was to act. He threw himself past the tree, then around it in a lunge.

The loop caught him as he had known it would, but as the horse leaped to drag him he had a turn around the tree, then a second. The horse hit the end of the rope with a lunge and the girth parted. The horse charged on, then man, saddle and rope hit the ground hard.

Drako swore and the third man grabbed for a gun.

Shanaghy never knew how he did it but he had not stopped moving. When the girth broke he had thrown off the rope and when the third man grabbed for his gun, Shanaghy shot him.

He intended to shoot him through the body but the man was moving and the bullet caught his left arm at the elbow, breaking it.

"Next time," Shanaghy covered his miss, "I'll break the other arm. Now get out of here . . . all of you."

"Mister?" The man with his hands behind him spoke softly, desperately. "Mister, I never begged for anything in my life, but—"

For the first time Shanaghy realized that the man's hands were tied behind his back.

"Leave that man here," Shanaghy said. "Let go that lead-rope and leave him."

"I'll be damned if I will!" Drako shouted.

"You'll be dead if you don't," Shanaghy replied. "I was mindin' my own affairs. You come bargin' in here an' you just tried to sweep too many streets all to once. If you want to live long enough to see sundown you'll get out, and if you come back you'll deserve what you get."

"Oh, we'll be back, all right!"

Drako dropped the lead-rope and turned his horse away. "We'll surely be back!"

Shanaghy watched them ride away and then he walked over to the bound man and cut his hands loose. "Don't know what they had you for, chum," he said, "but that's a bad lot."

The man rubbed his wrists. "You're new in this country," he replied grimly. "They was fixin' to hang me. If you hadn't been here I'd be dead by now."

Shanaghy walked to the tree where he had concealed his blanket-roll and the shotgun, and took them up.

"My name's Tom Shanaghy," he said.

"Josh Lundy," the older man said. Then he added, "We got but one horse. No use killin' him carryin' double. You ride awhile, then I will."

Lundy reached for the bed-roll but stopped abruptly, his eyes on the shotgun. Then slowly he took the roll of blankets and tied it behind the saddle. "You carry a shotgun all the time?" he asked. Something in his tone drew Shanaghy's attention.

"No . . . Why?"

"Wondered."

Yet suddenly Lundy's manner had changed. The friendliness was gone from his tone and he was somehow cool and remote.

"You come far?" he asked suddenly.

"New York."

"On a train, you said?"

"Uh-huh. Railroad bull bounced me off back yonder a ways. I walked for awhile, then saw this stream and followed her to here."

"Got you an outfit there. Didn't figure you fellers in New York carried blanket-rolls."

"We don't."

"You were almighty quick with that gun," Lundy said. "I never seen a man no quicker."

"Fellow taught me. I never used a gun very much. Where I come from it's knuckle-and-skull, the boots if you go down."

Tom Shanaghy was used to walking and he stepped off briskly. He was puzzled by all that had happened and

waited for Lundy to explain, which he seemed in no hurry
to do. In fact, since seeing the shotgun he had said very
little.

Shanaghy looked around as he walked. As far as he
could see there was nothing but grass and sky and the
twin ruts of the trail cutting through the grass ahead.
Here and there along the road there were sunflowers in
bloom.

He paused suddenly. "Lundy, what in God's name do
they do with all this country? There's no farms."

"Cattle country," Lundy replied, "grazin' land. Used
to be buffalo."

Something moved in the distance, a moment of tawny-
red when caught by the sun's rays, then a flicker of white
and they were gone.

"What was that? Cows?"

"Antelope," Lundy said. "There's a good many of them."

"Who they belong to?"

Lundy glanced at him. "God, I guess you could say.
They're wild."

"Can you hunt them?"

"Uh-huh. Not the best eatin' though. They're good
enough, but not so good as buffalo or deer meat." He
walked the horse in silence for several minutes and then
asked, "What do you aim to do now?"

"Me? Catch a train back to New York. I piled on that
train in a hurry and I was dead tired. I never wanted to
get this far away." He hesitated, suddenly thoughtful. "Say,
how far is it to New York, anyway?"

Lundy shrugged. "You got me. Maybe a thousand
miles."

Shanaghy pulled up short. "A thousand . . . ? It can't
be!"

"It is. Maybe more. This here's Kansas you're in."
Lundy pointed ahead. "Colorado's right over there. You
must have been really knocked out when you hit that
train."

"Well . . . I'd been movin' a lot. Hadn't slept much, that's
true. I was dead beat." He scowled, thinking back. "I
woke up now and again but it seems the train was always
movin'. One time I looked out and there was nothing but
four or five buildings across the street and some riders . . .
I don't know where that was."

"Least, you had you an outfit."

Shanaghy offered no reply. He was growing increasingly uneasy. The best thing he could do was get to a station and buy a ticket for New York. There, at least, he knew what was going on.

"Those lads back yonder," he said suddenly, "what were they going to hang you for?"

"I stole a horse. That's hanging out here. But this one I stole back. Belongs to a girl-kid. That Drako . . . he wanted the horse."

"The girl got the horse now?"

"Uh-huh."

Shanaghy looked at the saddle. "That's a heavy piece there. That saddle, I mean."

"Stock saddle. It's a work saddle. A man handlin' cattle and rough stock needs a good saddle to work from and this here's the best. Most cowhands spend most of their lives settin' in saddles just like this.

"I seen some of those eastern saddles . . . like postage stamps. They're all right for somebody who spends an hour or so in the saddle, but a cowhand is up in the leather sixteen to eighteen hours a day. He's roping stock from the saddle and needs a pommel where he can either tie fast or take a turn, depending on how he was raised and where he learned his business. A saddle is a cowhand's work-bench."

Lundy pulled up. " 'Bout time you took a turn, although I ain't much at walkin'."

Shanaghy mounted and settled himself in the strange saddle. It felt good. The seat was natural, and although the stirrups were longer than he was used to he did not take time to shorten them.

"Town up ahead," Lundy commented, after awhile. "You keep that gun handy. Drako may be around. That's a rough crew he runs with and they don't like anybody messing with them."

"What about you?"

"When we get close to town I'm goin' to cut an' run. I've got friends there, somebody who'll lend me a gun. I ain't huntin' trouble. You being a stranger . . . you be right careful. From what I've heard they fight with fists back east. Well, out here it's like in the South. We settle our troubles with guns."

Shadows were long when they rode into town. Shanaghy was again in the saddle when they reached the town's edge and he stepped down. "Here's your horse, Lundy," he said. "See you around."

"Shanaghy?" Lundy hesitated a moment as if reluctant to speak. "Better keep that shotgun out of sight. Somebody will recognize it."

"Recognize it? How?"

"I don't know how you come to have it," Lundy said, "but that shotgun is known by sight in at least twenty towns out here. That shotgun belonged to Marshal Rig Barrett."

"I never heard of him."

"Well, ever'body out here has. Rig was his own army. When he moved into a place folks knew he was there. He cleaned up towns, outlaw gangs, train robberies, whatever. And he never let anybody even handle one of his guns."

"So?"

Josh Lundy gathered the reins and stepped into the saddle. "Marshal Rig Barrett had a lot of enemies, Shanaghy. He had a lot of friends, too. And they are going to be asking questions and wanting answers."

Lundy looked up the dusk-filled street. He wanted to be away, but he stalled. "Shanaghy," his tone sharpened with irritation, "don't you see? They're going to want to know how you came by Rig's shotgun. They're going to tell themselves the only way you could lay hands on it would be over Rig's dead body, and they just aren't going to believe any eastern pilgrim could kill Rig in a fair fight."

"I didn't kill him. I never so much as saw him."

"Who's going to believe that?"

"Nobody will have to. I'll be out of town on the next train. This town will never see hide nor hair of me again."

"If they see that shotgun and figure you killed Rig, you'll never get a chance to leave. They'll hang you, boy. They'll give you the rope they planned to use on me."

"When's the next train leave? You know this town."

"Nothing out of here in either direction until tomorrow noon, and that one is west-bound. There will be an east-bound train tomorrow evening about nine o'clock."

Lundy turned his horse and rode off. When he had

gone about fifty feet he called back. "Was I you I'd not wait for that evening train."

Tom Shanaghy stood alone in the dusty street and swore, slowly, bitterly. Then he unrolled the blankets, took down the shotgun, and rolled it up again.

He would get something to eat, then a ticket and a bed.

# Chapter IV

It was suppertime in town and the streets were almost empty. Not that there was much to the town, only a row of stores, saloons, gambling joints and a hotel or two facing a dusty street from either side. Here and there were hitching rails and there were boardwalks in front of most of the buildings.

He walked to what looked like the best hotel and went in. The clerk, a tall young man with a sallow face and hollows over his cheekbones, pushed the ledger toward him. He signed it *Thomas Shanaghy, New York,* and pushed it back.

"That will be fifty cents, Mr. Shanaghy. Will you be staying long?"

"Until the east-bound train tomorrow night," Shanaghy said.

He paid for the room with a ten-dollar gold piece and received his change.

"If you are interested in a little game, Mr. Shanaghy," the clerk suggested, "there's one going in the back room right here in the hotel."

"Thanks," Shanaghy had been a shill himself and was not to be taken in. "I never gamble."

"No? Then perhaps—"

"I don't want a girl, either," Shanaghy said. "I want something to eat, some rest, and a New York newspaper if you've got one."

The clerk did not like him very much. He jerked his thumb toward a door from which there was an occasional rattle of dishes. "You can eat in there." He indicated the opposite direction. "And there's a saloon over there. As for a New York newspaper . . ."

He shuffled through some newspapers on the desk, all well-read by the looks of them. "I am afraid we haven't

42

any. Occasionally some drummer leaves one in the lobby, so you might look around."

Shanaghy considered that and decided against it. He took his key, listened to the directions of the clerk and took up his blanket-roll and went up the stairs. Chances are there would be nothing about the New York gambling war in the paper anyway, he decided. There were always brawls, gang-fights and killings, and the newspapers reported only a small percentage of them. John Morrissey was a popular figure, of course, but Eben Childers was scarcely known away from the Five Points, the Bowery and a scattering of places in the vicinity of Broadway.

The room offered little. A window over the street, a bed, a chair, a dressing table with an oval mirror, and on the table beneath the mirror a white bowl and pitcher. There was water in the pitcher. On a rack beside it there was a towel.

On the floor there was a strip of worn carpet. Shanaghy removed his coat, rolled up his sleeves and bathed his face and hands, then put water on his hair and combed it.

He studied himself critically. At five-nine he was a shade taller than average, and he was stronger than most, due to the hard work in the smithys. The girls along the Line were always telling him how handsome he was, but that was malarkey. They knew he was a friend of Morrissey's and the Morrissey name stood for power and influence in the world they knew, so they were always buttering him up. Not that he saw much of them. He had always been on the gambling, roughneck side.

Brushing his coat with his hands, he put it on and picked up his hat and went down the stairs. The restaurant was open, and he went in, ordered some beef and beans and began to relax.

The waiter was a portly man with slicked-back hair who wore a candy-striped shirt and sleeve-garters. He filled Shanaghy's cup and slopped a liberal portion into the saucer.

A screened window was open on the street and Shanaghy heard the clang of a blacksmith's hammer. He jerked his head toward the sound. "Workin' late, ain't he?"

"Lots of work," the waiter put down the coffeepot. "Soon be time for the cattle drives, too. There's always riders who need horses shod when the drives are on. He keeps busy."

The waiter took his pot and moved away and Shanaghy relaxed slowly. It felt good just to sit. For days now . . . weeks, actually, he'd been on the go. Now he had nothing to do until this time tomorrow night. He'd better buy that ticket right away. If anything happened he would at least have his ticket, and once in New York again he'd be all right.

What could happen? He shrugged a shoulder in reply to his own question and looked up to see the waiter returning with a steaming plate. "If you want more, sing out," the waiter said. "We're used to hungry men."

Shanaghy was halfway through his meal when the door from the street opened and a man came in, spurs jingling. He crossed to a table where two other men sat eating. Pulling back a chair he dropped into it. "Ain't no sign of him," the newcomer said. "He's three days overdue. That ain't like Rig."

Shanaghy was cutting a piece from his steak, and at the name he almost stopped.

Rig? Rig Barrett?

"Last word we had he was in Kansas City. That was last week."

"He may be here, scoutin' around. You know how he is, never makes any fuss."

"I'm worried, Judge. You know what Vince Patterson said, and Vince ain't a man who blows off a lot of hot air. Last I heard he was hirin' hands down around Uvalde and Eagle Pass, tough hands. Joel Strong rode in a few days ago and he said Vince had hired twenty-five men . . . Now you know he doesn't need more than half that many to bring twenty-five hundred head over the trail. So why's he hirin' so many men?"

"Maybe worried about Indians."

"Him? Vince would tackle hell with a bucket of water. No, this time he figures to get even. When his brother was killed, Vince promised us he'd be back."

"He can't blame the whole town for that."

"He does, though. Vince is a tough man and he doesn't fool around. Rig Barrett could make him see the light, but you know and I know that Vince won't back down for no man."

The judge sipped his coffee, then lit a cigar. "I know Vince. He's a hard man, all right. It takes hard men to do what he did. He came out from Kentucky and started roping and branding cattle. He made friends with some Indians, fought those who wanted to fight, and he built a ranch. He worked all by himself, the first two years. Then his brother came out and worked and fought right beside him. That was the brother Drako killed."

Drako?

Tom Shanaghy heard only snatches of the conversation from there on, no matter how he strained his ears. He was curious, naturally. Rig Barrett had evidently planned on riding that freight west and somehow had gotten off again and left his gear behind . . . But why should such a man ride a freight? To come into town unseen? Maybe, but Rig didn't seem like a man who would care. He might even want the townspeople to see him arrive.

So what had become of him? Shanaghy wished there was a train that night. Right away. He began to feel hemmed in. His old friend of the shooting galleries had told him much about the West. If you shot a man in a fair fight there was no argument. If you shot a man in the back, or murdered him otherwise, you could get hung. You had a choice . . . run or be hung.

If Shanaghy was found with the shotgun and blanket-roll that belonged to Rig, he would be presumed guilty.

He finished his coffee and got up, then paid for his meal and left. Two-bits . . . Well, that wasn't too bad. And the food was good.

The air was fresh and cool in the street and there were few people about. The sound of the blacksmith's hammer drew him forward and he strolled down the street.

The wide doors of the shop were pushed back. The fire on the forge glowed a dull red, and there were several lanterns hung about to give light. The smith glanced up as Shanaghy stepped into the door.

"Workin' late," Shanaghy commented. "Buy you a drink?"

"Don't drink."

"Well, neither do I. Have one now and again." He glanced at the work the smith was doing. "Makin' a landside? I haven't made one of those in years. Seen my pa do it many's the time."

"Are you a smith?"

"Now and again. My pa was a good one."

"Want a job?"

Shanaghy hesitated. "I'm leavin' town tomorrow night,

but if you're crowded with work I could work nine, ten hours tomorrow. What is it, mostly?"

"Shoeing horses, a couple of wagons to fit with new tires, some welding."

"I can do that. I'm not experienced with plows or plowshares. I've been living in New York City and it has been mostly shoeing driving or riding horses . . . putting tires on a few wagons and buggies."

"You come in at six o'clock, you've got a day's work. Wish you could stay. I've got enough work for three men, and everybody wants his work done right now."

The smith mopped his brow. "Here," he pulled an old kitchen chair around. "Time I took a rest. You set for awhile. New York, eh? I've never been there."

"You got you a tire-bender?"

"Heard of them. Are they any good?"

"Some of them. I never saw one until last year, but a mighty good smith I worked with in New York, name of McCarthy, he used one. Liked it."

"Maybe I should get one. Might save some time."

"Been smithing here long?"

"Long? Hell, I started this town! Man down the road a piece saw my gear when I was passin' along the trail, and he asked me if I could bend a tire. Well, I did four wagons for him, and meanwhile several people brought horses to be shod.

"Out here folks do most of their own shoeing, but it leaves a lot to be said for it. Most of them do a pretty slam-bang job of it.

"Well, I worked there for about two weeks and then I moved back under that big cottonwood, and between times I put up a shed. Then old Greenwood came along with a wagon loaded with whiskey, and he pulled in and began peddling drinks off the tailgate of his wagon.

"I'd taken the trouble to claim a quarter-section, so he was on my land. I told him so and he made me no argument but started paying rent. Then Holstrum came in, and he found where my quarter ended and filed on the quarter-section right alongside. He put in his store and we had a town.

"Today we've got the stockyards and the railroad, so there's eighty-odd people livin' here now."

"Much trouble?"

"Some . . . Them Drakos are trouble. They settled

down over west of here. There's the old man and three, four boys. Unruly. That's what they are, unruly. Greenwood, Holstrum an' me, why we want this here to be a *town*. We got it in mind to build a church and a school . . . maybe both in one building until we can manage more.

"We made a mistake there at the beginning. We chose Bert Drako for marshal and he straightened out a few bad ones who drifted in . . . killed one man.

"Then it kind of went to his head. That killing done it, I guess. He's got to thinking he's the whole cheese hereabouts. Him and those boys of his. They've begun to act like they owned the town, and we don't need that. Don't need it a-tall! This here's a good little town.

"Four or five of us got together and formed ourselves a committee. We've transplanted several small trees to start a park, and we're diggin' a well in our spare time . . . a town well, and then one for the park, too."

He got up. "Well, back to work. If you're still of a mind to do some smithing, you come around. I'll be in here shortly after sun-up."

Tom Shanaghy walked back uptown and stopped in front of the hotel. For a moment he stood there, looking up and down the dim street, lighted only here and there by windows along the way.

He shook his head in disbelief. This was a *town?* It was nothing, just a huddle of ramshackle frame buildings built along a railroad track, with nothing anywhere around but bald prairie. Yet the smith had sounded proud, and he seemed to genuinely love the place. How, Shanaghy wondered, could anybody?

As for himself, he couldn't get out of it fast enough. He would help the smith tomorrow, as it would serve to pass the time. Besides, he liked the feel of a good hammer in his hand, the red-glow from the forge and the pleasure of shaping something, making something. Maybe that was why these people liked their town, because they had built it themselves, with their own hands and minds.

He went upstairs, turned in and slept well, with a light spatter of rain to aid his slumber and cool things off. Awakening in the morning he thought of the letters and papers in the blanket-roll. He should look at them, as there might be some clue in them as to Rig Barrett and what had happened to him.

The sun was not yet up, although it was vaguely gray outside. He lay still for awhile, gathering his wits and somewhat uncomfortable. The bed was good enough, and the fresh prairie air through the window was cool and pleasant. The discomfort, he realized, was only within himself, yet he could find no reason for it.

Oddly, New York, to which he would be returning, seemed far away and he had a hard time placing it all in his mind. Every time he tried to bring the city within focus, it faded out, and the feeling irritated him.

He bathed, dressed, prepared his things for a quick departure, and then went down to breakfast. The citizens of the town ate at home, and only transients such as himself ate at the hotel. On this morning there was only one other person in the dining room ... a young woman wearing a gray traveling outfit, a very cool and composed young woman who took him in at a glance and then ignored him.

She was quite pretty, an ash-blonde with very regular features. Obviously awaiting someone, she was impatient now, and she glanced often at a tiny watch she carried in her purse. Curious, Shanaghy took his time, wondering who she was to meet and what such a girl was doing in this place.

He knew little of women. Most of those he knew had been the girls off the Line or those who walked the streets on the Bowery, and he knew them only by sight or the casual contacts made in dance halls where he went often to collect for Morrissey, who owned several.

It was early for such a woman to be around. Had she come in from the country? That was unlikely. Had she got off a train? The first of the day had not arrived yet.

A new man entered. He was slim and dark, wearing a Prince Albert coat and a planter's hat. He was neat, his gray vest spotless, the striped gray pants hanging down over highly polished boots.

Shanaghy glanced at him. Though he had never seen the man before, he knew the type, a con-man and a four-flusher. He was smooth and handsome, with a face that seemed to have all the right lines but somehow missed something.

The girl started up, then sank back. "George! Of all people!"

She acted surprised, but Shanaghy was sure this was the person she had waited for. Why the act then?

Shanaghy refilled his cup. The smith could wait just a little longer.

# Chapter V

Whatever was happening here was none of his business, but Shanaghy knew breeding when he saw it, and the girl had it. The man did not. He was simply a flashy tough who had put on the outward manners of a gentleman, and Shanaghy knew that something was in the wind.

Seeming to be unaware of them, he accepted a plate of steak and eggs from last night's waiter. Scarcely had the waiter gone when Shanaghy heard George say, "Don't worry, ma'am. I promised you he'd never get here and he will not."

"But what if they get someone else?"

The man shrugged. "There's nobody else. Barrett had the reputation, and he knew how to handle such situations. With him out of the picture it will happen just as we want it to."

After that there was only an overheard word here and there, but Shanaghy understood nothing. Barrett must be Rig Barrett, but how could George be sure Rig would not show up?

The couple turned suddenly to look at him, but he was seemingly oblivious to their conversation and they could not know they had spoken loud enough to be overheard. Anyway, from Shanaghy's dress he was obviously not native to the town, but a stranger.

Despite himself, he was puzzled. Who were these people? Why was it important to them that Rig Barrett not be present? And how could George be so sure Rig would not show up . . . unless he had made sure he would not?

Murder? Why not, if the stakes were great enough? But what stakes could be, in such a place as this? Yet . . . Shanaghy didn't know. This country was new to him and he did not know where the money was.

Cattle, someone had said. Grazing land. There was a

shortage of beef in the eastern states. He had heard talk of that. Yet if it was cattle, where were they? And why was it necessary for Barrett to be out of the picture?

Tom Shanaghy was a cynic and a skeptic. The world in which he had lived in New York was a world where only the dollar counted. If people were after something, it had to be money or a commodity that could be turned into money. Such a girl as this was not meeting such a man unless there was money in it. No doubt she thought she was using him, and probably he believed he was using her.

Cattle came from Texas. Vince Patterson was coming up from Texas with cattle. He was coming to revenge himself upon the town where Drako had been marshal.

Hence it was possible that this girl was somehow connected with Patterson, or hoped somehow to profit from his arrival in town.

Too bad he was leaving for New York. He would like to see what happened.

He got up, paid for his meal and walked down the street to the blacksmith shop. The smith was using the bellows on his fire. "Couple of wheels to be fitted with tires," he commented. "Hank Drako's wagon. He brought it in last week and was mad when I wouldn't fit the tires right off. Now I know Hank. He fords three little streams coming in here, and in one of them he always pulls up in midstream to let his horses drink. So while he's settin' there those tires and wheels are soaking up water. You can't fit a tire unless the wheel is all dried out and I told him he'd have to leave it. He was mighty put out about it."

He pointed with his hammer. "There's the wheels. I made the tires. You go ahead and fit them."

Shanaghy took off his coat and shirt and hung them on nails inside the smithy. Then he built a circular fire outside in the yard at a place where such fires had been built before. When he had a small fire going, he laid the tire in it and put some of the burning sticks on top to get a more uniform heat.

After a few minutes he tried the iron with a small stick and, after a few minutes, tried it again. This time the stick slipped easily along the tire as if oiled, and a thin wisp of smoke arose from it.

In the meantime he had placed the wheel to be fitted

on a millstone, fitting the hub into the center hole. Putting the tire in position, Shanaghy pried it over the wheel with a tiredog, aided with a few hefty blows from a six-pound sledge. The tire went into place, the wood smoking from the heat of the iron tire, the wood of the wheel cracking and groaning as the tire contracted. The smith had a rack with a trough in which the wheel could be turned until the tire could be contracted to a tight fit. The cool water in the trough sloshed as he turned.

Shanaghy was busy with the second wheel when he heard a horseman ride up. He worked on, conscious of scrutiny, and when he finished driving the tire into place he added a few taps for good measure and then turned.

A thin, stoop-shouldered man with a drooping mustache sat a buckskin horse, watching him. The man wore an old blue shirt, homespun pants tucked into boots, and a six-shooter. He also carried a rifle in his hands. His hat was narrow-brimmed and battered.

"Ain't seen you before," he said.

"Good reason for it."

"What's that?" The man sat up a little, not liking Shanaghy's tone.

"I haven't been here before."

The man stared at him and Shanaghy went on about his work. He had some strap-hinges to make, and he went about it.

"You the pilgrim had the run-in with my son?"

Shanaghy looked up. He was aware that the smith was watching. So were a couple of men on the boardwalk across the street.

"If that was your son," Shanaghy suggested, "you'd better advise him not to try to take in too much territory. I was minding my own affairs."

"My son's my deputy. So was the man you shot."

"Deputy? You need deputies to handle a town this size?" Shanaghy straightened up from the anvil. "A man who couldn't handle a town this size by himself must be pretty small potatoes."

"What's that?" Drako reined his horse around threateningly. "You sayin' I don't amount to much?"

"Mister," Shanaghy said, "if I couldn't handle a town this size without deputies, I'd quit. Also, if I were you I'd advise your son that hanging a man without a trial is murder, no matter who does it."

Shanaghy thought he had Drako pegged, yet he knew he was taking a chance. For that he was prepared. Since childhood he had been facing boys and men, some of whom were tough, some who just believed they were. He did not like this Drako any more than he had liked his arrogant son, but it had never been his way to dodge a fight. He had discovered long since that such men accept dodging as cowardice and it only invited trouble.

One way or the other, he didn't care. Within hours he would be riding the cars back to New York, where enough trouble already awaited him.

"You talk mighty free," Drako said.

"Mister, I have work to do. If you've come here hunting trouble, step right in and get started. If you aren't hunting trouble, I'd suggest you get on down the street while you're all in one piece."

Shanaghy had a light hammer in his hand and he knew what he could do with it. Long ago he had learned how to throw a hatchet or a hammer with perfect accuracy. He knew that before Drako could put a hand on his gun, he could have that hammer on its way. And once thrown, Shanaghy would follow it in. It was a chancy thing to do, but he had been taking such chances all his life.

Drako hesitated, then reined his horse around. "I'll see you again!" he blustered, then rode off.

"You do that," Shanaghy called out. "Any time, any place."

The smith heaved a sigh when Drako was gone. "Figured he was goin' to shoot you," he said.

"And me with this hammer? I'd have put it right between his eyes."

"Just as well you're leavin' town," the smith said, "although I surely wish you weren't. You're the best I've seen in awhile. You must have you a girl back there to want to go so bad."

"A girl? No, I've no girl." Yet the thought reminded him of the girl in the gray traveling outfit.

"Speaking of girls . . ." Shanaghy began, then went on to describe her. "Do you have any idea who she is?"

"I surely don't, but I know she didn't come in on the train, like you'd expect. She rode in a-horseback . . . side-saddle. She rode in early so I doubt she came far."

The smith paused. "She's a handsome young woman. You interested in her?"

"Not that way. Kind of curious, though, about who she is and where she found that man she was talkin' to."

They returned to work. At noon, Shanaghy hung up the leather apron and washed his hands in the tub. As he dried them, he thought about the girl, Drako, and Barrett.

"Smithy," he asked, "this man Barrett, who has been sent for? What if he doesn't show?"

"There'll be hell to pay. Vince Patterson is a hard, hard man, and from all we hear he's coming up the trail loaded for bear. Short of a shooting war there's no way we can stop him. He knows how many men we've got and he will have more."

"And Rig Barrett could stop him?"

He shrugged. "Who knows? He could if anybody could. Rig's been there before, and they know it. He's a strong man, and they know if shooting starts somebody will die. Somebody may die anyhow, but with Rig shooting it's no longer a gambling matter.

"What we hope for is that he'll be here, and that his mere presence will stop them. He's a known man."

Later, when Shanaghy walked to the door to cool off in the light breeze, he looked down the street at the town and shook his head, wonderingly.

It was nothing. A collection of ramshackle shacks and frame buildings stuck up in the middle of nowhere, and yet men were willing to fight for it. He took out his heavy silver watch and looked at it. There were hours yet before the train was due.

The smith came out and stood beside him.

"It ain't much," Shanaghy said.

"It's all we've got," the smith replied. "And it's home."

*Home* . . . how long since he had a real home? Shanaghy wondered. His thoughts went back to the stone cottage on the edge of moors in Ireland. He remembered the morning walks through the mist when he went to the uplands to bring the horses down. How long ago it seemed! He turned away from the dusty street and walked back to the forge.

Yet the thoughts of home had altered his mood. He finished a lap weld in a wagon tire, and returned to making hinges, but suddenly he was feeling lost and lonely, remembering the green hills of Ireland and the long talks with his father beside the forge. His father, he realized now, had been a strange man, half a poet, half a mystic.

"A man," his father said once, "should be like iron, not steel. If steel is heated too much it becomes brittle and it will break, while iron has great strength, boy. Yet it can be shaped and changed by the proper hammering and the right amount of heat. A good man is like that."

What had Rig Barrett been like?

Shanaghy took a punch and made holes in a hinge, thinking about Barrett. The smith stopped, straightening up and putting a hand across the small of his back.

"This man Barrett," Shanaghy said. "Tell me about him."

The smith hesitated, thinking about it. "A small man," he said. "He rode with the Texas Rangers during the war with Mexico. Fought Comanches, drove a team over the Santa Fe Trail. As a boy, they tell me, he drove turkeys or pigs to market back east—drives that would go for more'n a hundred miles.

"He's been over the trail a time or two and folks know him. They know he's an honest man who will stand for no nonsense. We figured if anybody could make Vince Patterson see the light, why, he was it."

The smith glanced at him. "You're a good hand. Why don't you stay? What's back in New York that makes it so important?"

"New York? Hell, man, that's my town! I . . ." Shanaghy's voice trailed off. Who was he fooling? New York was not his town. Chances were, by now they'd forgotten all about him. In a country town like this if a man turned up missing, like Rig Barrett, for example, he left quite a hole. Back in New York, if one Irish slugger stepped out of line or got lost, somebody else stepped right into his place and nobody even remembered.

McCarthy might remember. Morrissey might even give him a thought.

"See here," the smith said suddenly. "You're a good man. If you didn't want to work for me, I could sell you a half-interest."

Shanaghy smiled. "I think not. I'd not make light of your town, Smith, but I am a city man. I like the lights and the bustle. Besides, if this Vince Patterson is all you say he is, your town may not be here much longer. That man who was talking to that young woman . . . I heard part of something this morning . . . I got the impression he didn't expect Rig to ever get here."

The smith had turned back to the forge, but now he turned sharply around. "What's that mean?"

"Well," Shanaghy replied lamely, "I can't really say. Maybe they were talking about somebody else, but I got the idea they were talking about Rig. I also got the idea that steps had been taken to see that he never got here."

The smith took off his apron. "You stay right here, Shanaghy. I've got to see a man."

The smith left, almost running.

"Now what the hell have you done?" Shanaghy asked himself. "You and your big mouth. You don't know anything, you're just surmising. And why should they care, anyway?"

The fact remained that they did care. Whatever that girl had in mind she cared a lot, and so had the man with her. They had not wanted Rig Barrett to be around when Vince Patterson reached town. Shanaghy took out a big silver watch. It was still hours until train time.

Well, this was the town's problem, if it could be called a town. He took up another set of hinges and placed them on the pile, then started all over again. He liked the feel of the hammer in his hand, checking the heat of the iron on which he worked by the color.

He walked to the door and looked up and down the street. There were two buggies and a wagon standing at the hitching-rails. Several horses, saddled, were tied along the street, usual, he supposed, for this time of day.

Suddenly the man called George appeared on the street. He glanced up and down, then strolled slowly along, lingering here and there as if to see into the various stores. When he reached the blacksmith shop he paused and taking a thin cigar from his pocket, he lighted it, glancing at Shanaghy.

"Where's the smith?" he asked.

"Around."

"Back soon?"

"Soon. Can I do something for you?"

George smiled. His teeth were white, his smile pleasant. Yet only the lips smiled. The eyes were cool, calculating. "I didn't know the smith had a helper."

"Occasionally."

"You from around here?"

Shanaghy shrugged. "Who is? This is a new town, mister. Everybody here is from somewhere else. Like you . . . Where do you come from?"

George threw him a sharp, hard look. "I thought that was a question that wasn't asked out here."

"You asked me."

"Ah? So I did. Well, I'm from Natchez, on the Mississippi."

"Gambling town," Shanaghy commented. "At least Natchez-Under-the-Hill is. They tell me there are a lot of shysters and con-men around there . . . and more crooked gamblers than anywhere."

George's eyes took on a hard, ugly look. "It seems to me you know a good deal about Natchez. You've been there?"

"Heard about it."

"You hear too much."

Shanaghy suddenly felt good. He did not know why he felt so good, but he did. Maybe it was the prospect of a fight, or maybe it was because he simply did not like George.

He looked at George, and he smiled.

Angered, George turned sharply away, yet he had not taken two steps before Shanaghy spoke.

Why he said what he did he would never know. It would have been wiser to let well enough alone, yet the words came out uncalled for.

"Really doesn't make much difference whether Rig comes or not," he said. "Everything's ready."

# Chapter VI

George stopped so abruptly it was a wonder he didn't fall on his face. He turned slowly and for a moment they stared at each other.

George, Shanaghy reflected, did not like him. He didn't like him at all. Yet George's tone was even. "Who was that you mentioned? Rig, did you say?"

"Rig Barrett," Shanaghy said, "a careful man. Leaves nothing to chance."

He didn't know what he was talking about, but he didn't like George any better than the gambler, or whatever he was, liked him, and he spoke merely to irritate him. Yet there was more, for the townspeople were worried about Vince Patterson and George, he knew, was somehow connected with all that might happen.

Most of the people he had known made crime a profession, and there were many such around the Bowery, the Five Points and lower Broadway. Many believed all honest men to be stupid, and usually were overly optimistic about their own plans, believing they couldn't fail. Nor did they ever seem to realize they were risking their lives or, at the very least, several years of their lives against sums of money that could in no way pay for the time they were losing or the pleasures they would be missing.

The man called George was such a one, sure that he was much smarter than those with whom he dealt. And even when he was being used, he would be certain he was using them. But who was the girl? What was her part in all this?

"Rig Barrett? I don't believe I know him." George's left hand unbuttoned his coat. "Is he from around here?"

"Figured you knew him," Shanaghy replied blandly.

58

"Everybody's talking about him. Folks seem to be expecting trouble when the cattle come up the trail, and they're figuring on Rig to handle it. If he gets here, that is. Personally, I think he's just keeping out of sight until the right moment, as he's not the kind of man to let people down."

George shrugged and turned away. "Sometimes a man can't help it," he suggested.

Shanaghy picked up his hammer again and went to the forge. He looked at the iron heating there. He put down the hammer, took the tongs and lifted the iron from the fire.

"A man like that," he said, "if he couldn't make it, would surely send somebody in his place."

George walked away, ignoring him, and Shanaghy chuckled, continuing with his work. He was punching holes in a hinge when a man came from across the street and stopped in the door.

"Where's Carpenter?"

"Carpenter?"

"The smith."

"Oh? I didn't know his name. Just called him Smith."

The man nodded. "Many do. Where is he?" He stepped forward, holding out his hand. "I'm Holstrum."

Shanaghy held up his. It was black with soot. "Sorry. I'm Tom Shanaghy. I've just been lending a hand here for a few hours."

"Glad to have you. We need good men."

"Drako still the marshal?"

"He is."

"Best fire him then, if Vince Patterson is hunting him. You'd best find a man the town will stand behind."

"Rig Barrett will fire him. Then there won't be any gunplay. We don't need any shooting."

"And if Rig doesn't get here?"

Holstrum hesitated, not enjoying the thought. Then he looked across the street, his face blank. "I will do it," he said. "It must be done before Vince Patterson arrives. Maybe if Drako had been fired, that will be an end to it, and if there is trouble let Drako handle it. He's been hunting trouble ever since the shooting."

"Suppose," Shanaghy wondered, "if Rig sent somebody in his place?"

"It wouldn't work. There is no other who would do as well. Rig is known. Perhaps Hickok . . . I do not know."

Shanaghy walked back to the bellows and worked at it, heating up the fire. "You can't know what will happen, Mr. Holstrum. Nor if Barrett will come. You had best be rid of Drako and have another marshal."

Holstrum shook his head. "That's the trouble. There are brave men here, but none of us are experienced at the handling of such trouble. All of us will fight, but it is not a fight we want. If there is shooting, there will be killing, and the more shooting the more killing. It is a job for Rig Barrett."

He paused. "There must be no trouble, for there are other herds coming, and there will be much business here and our town is young. We must have that business."

Holstrum walked back to the forge and watched the glowing embers, and the irons heating. "The cattle-buyers will come on the noon train, and they will be buying the herds that come over the trail. In the next few weeks there will be two or three hundred thousand dollars paid for cattle, and the cattlemen will pay off their hands. And many of them will buy clothing, food, supplies, liquor, whatever they need in our stores. Such money will put the town on a solid footing. We will be able to build our church and our school."

Shanaghy took the iron in the tongs and walked back to the anvil. He took up his hammer. He struck a blow, then another. He stopped. "Two or three hundred thousand dollars? Where would a town this size get that much money?"

"Oh, we don't have that much! Not by far. But we have sent for it and it will be here. We must pay off the drovers, you know, and the buyers will want checks cashed, and—"

"Two or three hundred thousand? It is coming by train?"

"How else? It will be here, and Rig Barrett is coming with it. I tell you, there must be no trouble."

Holstrum walked away and Shanaghy went on about his business. There was no bank in the town, although there was a building in which some ambitious person had painted

"BANK" a sign, no doubt with the best of intentions. Banking, such as there was, was handled by Holstrum himself or by Greenwood. No doubt the money for cashing checks written by the cattle-buyers would come from the safe of one or the other.

Carpenter did not return, so Shanaghy continued to work. One of the things he had always enjoyed about blacksmithing was the time to think. Once a man knew what he was doing, he could work swiftly, smoothly, and there was time to ponder.

The smith was a good man with tools—not so good as either McCarthy or his father, but good enough. He laid out his work well, and Shanaghy fitted two more rims to wheels and added to the supply of hinges.

In the corner of the room, fastened to a timber brace, he found a soot-stained sheet of paper listing work to be done. He studied it, then went ahead with what was needed, but his thoughts kept reverting to the girl in the restaurant and to George. What did they want? What were they after? Surely, the two could not be . . . no . . . whatever she was, she was not that type. Larceny maybe, prostitution, no.

The more he considered the situation, the surer he was that somehow or other George had contrived that Rig Barrett not be present when Patterson arrived with his cattle.

Was Barrett dead? Even the shrewdest of gunfighters can be shot from ambush . . . especially if it were done at some unexpected time or place. He thought again of the letters, the map in his pack. They would surely tell him something of where Barrett had been and what he had been doing.

Why a map?

Shanaghy had no answer to that. Suddenly he was restless. He must look at those letters.

Why had he not read them before? He hesitated over the answer to that, and then admitted that he felt a curious reticence about invading the privacy of another person.

A gentleman, his father had told him once, did not read another person's mail. Whatever these letters were, they were not addressed to him but to Rig Barrett . . . Yet Rig Barrett was not here, or didn't seem to be, and this was an emergency. He knew little of Barrett except what he heard, but he tried to put himself in Barrett's place.

What would Rig do? What would John Morrissey do? What would his father have done?

They would read those letters and plan accordingly. Look at the situation, Shanaghy told himself. These people expect Barrett. He has not come. George believes he will not or cannot come. Yet Shanaghy himself had Barrett's clothing, his blankets and his prized shotgun.

Damn it, he swore softly. Where are you, Carpenter?

He worked, but as he worked he wondered where George was and where that girl was. He also thought of those cattle with twenty-five tough cowhands moving north, mile by mile, coming closer and closer to that inevitable hour.

And what about Drako? Drako would also know of that, he and his tough sons. What were they doing? Were they going to run or fight?

Fight, he decided. They were too proud or too foolish to run. But they would need help . . . and probably knew where to get it.

At last Carpenter returned, and Holstrum was with him.

Shanaghy stripped off his apron. "Got to go up the street," he said. "I'll be back."

"Wait just a minute," Carpenter suggested. He turned to the storekeeper. "Holstrum, you tell him."

"Shanaghy, we don't know you, except that Carp here says you're a mighty fine smith and a good worker. He also says you backed down Drako."

Shanaghy shrugged. "I wouldn't say that. Drako likes to know who he's fightin', and I'm kind of unknown. He wasn't scared . . . He just wanted to think it over some. Just the same," he paused, "I don't think Drako is as tough as he'd like to have people think, or as tough as he'd like to believe he is."

"Nonetheless, you stopped him. He stood off when you showed yourself ready. Now, we've been expecting Rig Barrett and something's happened, because he hasn't showed."

"I don't think he's going to show," Shanaghy said.

They looked at him, suddenly attentive. Tom remembered, too late, about Josh Lundy's warning.

"I heard this man George tell a woman he wouldn't show." It sounded weak, he knew. There was suspicion in their eyes now.

"How could he know that?" Holstrum asked.

"He couldn't . . . unless he knew somebody had made certain of it." Shanaghy hung up the apron, took down his shirt and put it on. The two men watched him until he donned his coat, then somewhat reluctantly Holstrum suggested, "Shanaghy, I don't know you but Carpenter has respect for you, and he liked the way you stood off Drako. Well . . . if Rig doesn't show, how about you? Would you take on the job? Rig being a known man, he had the battle half won. It will be tougher for you."

Shanaghy smiled. What would Old Smoke say to that? Offered a job as marshal! Old Smoke, he realized suddenly, would have taken it, and he would have been right out there in the street to stop them. John Morrissey never backed water for any man. And come to think of it, he never had either. He'd run a couple of times, but only from numbers and when he knew he was coming back.

"Thanks," he said. "I have a ticket on the night train. I'm heading back to New York, where I've trouble enough waiting and some old scores to pay."

"Shanaghy," Holstrum protested, "we're in serious trouble here. Patterson's liable to burn our town. He has said he would."

"Sorry. When that train goes, I'll be on it."

He walked away up the street. Damn it, this wasn't his fight! What did they take him for? He just showed up in town and . . . What did they know about him, after all? And if they did know about him, what would they think then? It was like McCarthy said, he was nothing but a Bowery thug. Would they want him for marshal if they knew that?

Shanaghy went to his room and opened the haversack. For the first time he looked at the shirts. They were much too small for him, with his seventeen-inch neck. The cuffs were frayed and worn. Mr. Rig Barrett did not make much of being a peace officer, for the outfit was that of a poor man. Only the guns were neat and well-kept.

If Rig Barrett had been less than an honest man,

these shirts might have been made of the striped silk the gamblers wore—or some of them, at least.

Shanaghy took out the packet of letters, the notebook with the loose papers tucked inside, and the map. He put them down on the bed, then walked over and locked the door. He took out his six-shooter and placed it on the bed beside him as he sat.

There were four letters in the packet, and he put them aside, reluctant to open them. First, he looked at the loose papers.

The first was a carefully written description of the town, all compressed into about three lines, with a list of the stores, saloons and other buildings, and a diagram showing their locations along the street.

Below it were brief written outlines of several people, the first being: *Patterson, Vincent, age 36, height five feet ten inches, hair brown, eyes brown. M. Marcella Draper, 2 sons, 1 daughter. Father to Texas with Moses Austin. Mexican War 1 yr. service; Texas Rangers, 2 yrs. Veteran several Indian battles. Runs about 6,000 head. Rarely drinks, Strong, stubborn, fearless. Never leaves a job incomplete. Honest, a driver of men but feeds them well. Always has the best cook on the range. Excellent stock in remuda. Cattle always top grade. Can be reasoned with if in the mood. Once started, no stopping.*

*Drako, Henry, age 41, five feet eleven inches, black hair, mixed gray. Mustache, often unshaven. Believed wanted in West Virginia for horse theft; 3 sons, Win, Dandy, and Wilson. No record on boys. Suspected horse theft. Cattle theft. Movers. W. Va. to Ohio; to Illinois; served in Blackhawk War; to Tennessee, trouble with man named Sackett whose horse Drako "borrowed." Sackett recovered horse, suggested they leave. They did. Marshal killed V. Patterson's brother. Victim apparently under the influence.*

*Pendleton, Alfred. Brn Suffolk, Eng. Age 44 yrs. Six feet. Hair blond, eyes blue, slender build; 1 son, 1 daughter. Widower. Buys cattle, feeds, ships. Occasional buyer from Patterson. Win Drako suspected of stealing Pendleton calves. Quiet man, avoids trouble. Son, Richard, strong, athletic, attended William & Mary College 2 years. Now 25. Good horseman, good shot. Pendleton suffered reverses due to drouth, cattle theft.*

There were brief listings on Carpenter, Greenwood

and Holstrum that told Shanaghy nothing he did not already know. There were notes on several other businessmen and, at the end:

*Josh Lundy, cowhand, five feet eight inches, slender, age 29. Brn Texas. Presently employed by Pendleton. Witness in cow theft against Win Drako. Claimed horse in possession of Drako was stolen from Pendleton range, horse Lundy said owned by Jan Pendleton.*

That must be the horse Lundy had been accused of stealing. He said he had stolen a horse, stolen it back, for a girl.

*Lundy's father killed by Indians when he was twelve, supported mother and three sisters herding cattle, raising a few on his own. Wounded in Indian fight. Wounded again in fight with border bandits. Cattle drive to east, swam herd over the Mississippi. Right arm broken when thrown from bad horse. Good man with a rifle. Short arm makes handling pistol difficult. Reliable.*

Obviously, Rig Barrett was no fool and left little to chance. He wished to know what kind of men he must deal with.

Pendleton . . . Why did that name hold his attention? Lundy might have mentioned it when he spoke of stealing the horse. Jan Pendleton was obviously that girl.

The second page was a simple list of expenditures for supplies, ammunition and such items, along with a note of fifty dollars sent to "Maggie."

A third sheet was the beginning of a letter to Mag, evidently Barrett's wife:

*Dear Lady:*

*I taken pen in hand to inform you of my whereabouts and destination. Unfortunately, the prairie town to which I go offers employment for two months only, making it impractical to send for you, Dear Lady. I shall ride down the trail to meet Mr. Patterson before he is close to town. Perhaps we may reach an understanding.*

*The trouble I foresee will not come from him. There are other elements entering into this, which accounts for my presence in Kansas City. Be assured that when this task is complete I shall come to you at once, in St. Louis.*

*Do you remember Mr. Pendleton? The gentle-*

*man who loaned you the handkerchief on the train?*
*He is here—in the town, that is—and, I fear, is hav-*
*ing trouble.*
    *I shall write aga . . .*

The letter ended there and Tom Shanaghy put it down
with the others. It wasn't much help except to indicate
that Barrett had not anticipated trouble from Patterson
that he couldn't handle. What worried him was apparently something he had apparently come upon in Kansas City, or something that led him to go there.

What?

Shanaghy glanced through the packet of letters, but
none of them seemed of consequence. They were from
friends and business associates, but offered no clue to
what might have been the trouble in Kansas City.

There was one other note, another unfinished letter
written by Barrett to somebody:

    *I shall not ride the cushions, as I did before. This*
*time I'll speak to a conductor I know and arrange to*
*ride a caboose into town. That way I might arrive*
*unseen . . .*

Shanaghy put the letters down, and glanced at the
notebook. Probably nothing there but he would have
to see. The trouble was, he was hungry. He had been up
since daylight and had put in a hard morning's work
at the smithy. Yet he sat still, thinking.

Tom Shanaghy had never considered himself a
bright man. He had not even thought about it. He had
survived in a hard, rough world along the Bowery and
in the Five Points, and he supposed he was shrewd after
a fashion. Most of his problems he had solved with his
fists, but they did not help much now.

Rig Barrett, now, how about him? Barrett was supposed to be here and was not. Yet he was the kind of
man to keep appointments. Hence he was either here
and hiding out somewhere, or he was not here. If he
was not here, he must be unable to be here. And that
meant he was either a prisoner, which was unlikely, in-
jured or dead.

His gear had been on the train and in the gondola
in which Shanaghy was riding. That meant he had either

put the gear there himself, and had not followed it, or that the stuff had been thrown there by someone else.

Of course, Barrett might have gotten on the train and, for some reason, gotten off again. But that was unlikely, because if he had arranged to travel by caboose he would have gone directly to it.

"The way it looks," Shanaghy muttered, "is that Barrett was headed for the caboose when somebody laid one on him. Probably conked him on the noggin and then tossed his gear aboard a passing train, figuring to leave nothing that would name him when they found the body."

That also looks, he told himself, as though Mr. Rig Barrett is not going to arrive in town, and that means whoever plans to pull something off is going to have mighty little trouble doing it.

There was a sharp rap on the door. Shanaghy got to his feet and opened it.

Four men stood there and they all held guns. One of them was Holstrum. "They tell me," the big storekeeper said, "that you have Rig Barrett's shotgun."

Shanaghy glanced from one to the other. Nobody needed to tell him that he was in trouble. Just like Lundy had told him. He started to step forward and their guns lifted. One of them held a rope in his hand.

# Chapter VII

Tom Shanaghy was in trouble, but he had been in trouble before. He smiled, suddenly, thinking that he could remember few occasions when he had not been in trouble.

"That's right," he replied cheerfully, "I do have his shotgun. When he knew I was coming out here he said I might need it."

That was a lie, of course, but what he needed now was to keep himself from being hung, and he gave them the most likely story. They had already suggested that he might be the man to take Rig's place, so what better story than that Rig had actually sent him?

"Rig sent you? You know him?"

"Let's put it this way. Rig Barrett isn't here. I am. You need a man to take his place. I can do it. You want Drako fired, and I can do that, and will do it."

Shanaghy smiled again, at the thought. That, at least, he would enjoy doing.

"You mean to stop Vince Patterson?" Holstrum demanded. "You think you can?"

"It isn't Vince I'm worried about, gentlemen, nor was it Vince who worried Rig Barrett. Rig was quite sure he could talk to Vince and could reason with him. I mean to try the same thing."

"If he wasn't worried about Vince," Holstrum demanded, "then what did worry him?"

Now he had him. Rig had gone to Kansas City because of some suspicion he had, yet what that was Shanaghy did not know. He reached for the first thing that came to mind, and the moment it shaped into words Shanaghy was sure he had hit upon it.

"What worried him," Shanaghy paused, then suddenly decided to keep his mouth shut, "was something else entirely, but I am not free . . . I can't betray his confidence. Yet have no fear now. I shall handle it."

Yet all the time Shanaghy kept in mind that eastbound train that would get him out of all this. Would it come in time? Would he be able to get away?

Whatever else he had done, he had now made them unsure. So he spoke up with confidence. "Now, gentlemen, I am hungry. I want to eat and then get back to the smithy. But choose your time and if it is me you wish to be marshal here, let me know. I have work to do."

They turned to go and suddenly an idea came to Shanaghy. He said to Holstrum, "You know something of the railroad operations here. Is it customary to have a railroad detective riding the trains?"

Holstrum shook his head. "Never heard of such a thing. There's been no theft from freight cars, and we've had no goods lost."

When they were gone Shanaghy put his things together on the bed, then went down the stairs. This would be a good place to be away from if Rig Barrett did show up.

But that man who kicked him off the train? Just who was *he?*

"Shanaghy," he told himself, "you've come upon something. That was no railroad bull, that was somebody who wanted you off the train for fear of what you might see. And what might that have been, lad? What, indeed?"

Whoever he was, Shanaghy owed him one, but the thought nagged him that something was going on of which he knew nothing. Could that man have been tied in with George and the mysterious lady?

Carpenter himself was in the restaurant when Shanaghy entered. "Wife's sick," he said, "I'm eatin' out." He waved a hand and Shanaghy joined him. "Right where we sit I killed a buffalo, only last spring. Skinned him out right on the spot.

"Them times, there was nothing anywhere a man might look but grass waving in the wind. Now Holstrum has him a corn crop growing, and my wife has a vegetable garden. I tell you, my friend, this will be a town to be proud of!

"A few years ago some called this the Great American

Desert. They just didn't know soil! This here Kansas country will grow the finest corn, wheat and barley a man could wish for! You mark my words, one day this prairie where only buffalo ranged will feed half the world!

"We have been killing the buffalo. Magnificent as they are, a man must decide what his values are and you can grow no crops where buffalo range. There's no fence will stop them.

"My folks came from Europe and never owned a bit of land to call their own. They were beholden to the lord of the manor for their living, yet before my old father died he owned more than the lord of the manor had.

"You see a few poor shacks now, but give us time. We have been shipping buffalo hides and bones to the eastern markets, and now we're beginning to ship beef. Give us a few years and we will be storing and shipping grain."

He lifted a finger at Tom. "Shanaghy, we need young men here, young men like you."

"Like me?" Shanaghy's grin was sour. "What do you know of me?"

"All we need to know, all we will ever ask. You can do an honest day's work and you take pride in what you do. No man who loves the working of iron as you do can be bad."

Their food was brought and when the waiter had gone, Tom said, "The wheels you fitted for Drako? Beautiful! You're a fine craftsman, Tom! A fine craftsman!"

Shanaghy felt himslf flushing, and with pride, and embarrassment as well. Nobody had called him a craftsman before, and he relished the term.

"You take pride in your work. You have an eye for the color of red-hot iron such as only the true craftsman has.

"I tell you, Tom, a man who has never taken pride in a job well done is an empty man."

They ate then, and drank their coffee, but Carpenter had set Tom to thinking. Why not stay, after all?

What did he owe Morrissey, or any of them back east? Morrissey had given him a job when needed, but Tom had repaid him with an honest day's work and no shirking. He had fought Morrissey's enemies and made a few of his own in the process, but what had he to show for it? A little money in the bank, a tribute to his mother's advice.

Surely, there was not a soul there who would miss him past the week. Others had disappeared or gone away, and Shanaghy remembered well how little they were missed.

He could scarcely remember the Bowery for the grass blowing in the wind.

Carpenter put down his knife and fork. "Holstrum said you were taking the job as marshal, and that you were sent by Rig Barrett."

"In a way," Tom said, "and it doesn't look as if Rig is going to make it in time . . . . I shall do what he planned to do and ride out to meet Vince Patterson."

"You said you did not believe him to be the greatest trouble? What, then?"

"At this moment, I am not sure. I trust no man now, although you most of all."

"You won't be leaving on the train?"

Tom hesitated for a long time and then he said, "Not right now. Maybe later." He looked over at the smith. "I shall need a horse for a few days."

"I have one . . . the blue roan in the corral. There's the rig for him, too."

They went back to work then, and they handled their iron. And when the train came in, Tom was standing outside to see it stop. There was, he knew, still time. He could still make it. For a moment he hesitated, then went back into the shop and took off his apron.

"South of here," he asked Carpenter, "are there any ranches?"

"Nothing this side of Texas that I know of. Holstrum has a place about seven or eight miles southeast. Nothing but a cabin, shed and a corral. He runs a few head down there and usually has some horses for riding."

"Who takes care of the stock?"

"He's got a man there, but the stock doesn't drift much because he has the best grass and water for miles. He's a canny man, Holstrum is. I've a place, too, but not as good as the one he found."

Carpenter considered the subject, then added, "Only

other place around is about ten miles west. There's a two-by-four saloon over there and about three dugouts. Drako lives about three miles south of it, he and his boys."

"Who makes me marshal?" Shanaghy asks. "If I am to do anything I'd better be wearing a badge . . . or have one."

"Greenwood. You go see him. It was him suggested Rig Barrett. Greenwood's had experience with tough towns. He held out for Barrett and I backed him."

"What about Holstrum?"

"He was worried we'd get a worse Drako. So were some of the others. I could see his point, because Drako is bad enough."

Greenwood was leaning in his bar in the empty saloon when Shanaghy walked in. He was a pleasant-looking man who seemed to be in his late thirties. He smiled a little when he saw Shanaghy. "Talked you into it, did they? I hoped they would."

Shanaghy took the badge Greenwood pushed toward him and pinned it on his shirt pocket. "First time I ever wore one of them," he said.

Greenwood smiled. "You'll wear it with pride, son. I know your kind."

"My kind?" Shanaghy turned his eyes on him. "Mr. Greenwood, I've been a shoulder-striker for John Morrissey."

"Then you're a tough man, and that's what we need. It was never my luck to know Old Smoke, but I saw him fight once. A rough man, a hard man, and a tricky one when it came to elections, but I never knew him to go back on his word, and I know you will be the same. If there is any way in which I can help, let me know."

Shanaghy hesitated. "I don't know who I can trust."

"Who did you trust in New York?"

"Nobody . . . Maybe McCarthy, the smith."

"Then trust nobody here, not even me. Son, in the job you're taking you will stand on your own feet. You will get little help and no thanks from most people. They want the law, but they fear it, too.

"If you need a posse or riflemen, they will be sworn in, but they won't like it. Many men in this town have used guns and some are quite expert. But what a marshal needs is not men who are good with guns, but for himself to be good with men, with handling men.

"Take my word for it, son, a marshal must be judged not by the number of men he has killed in line of duty, but by the tough men he has handled without using a gun, even without violence."

"I don't know whether I am up to it."

"You are. Trust your own judgment of men and of situations. You must stand or fall by your own decisions."

"I think I know who—"

Greenwood lifted a hand. "Don't tell me. Don't tell anybody. Keep it to yourself. Gather your own facts, act upon them as you see fit. If you make a mistake you may be crucified for it. That's the job."

"Thanks."

"Let me buy you a drink," Greenwood suggested.

Shanaghy shook his head. "I don't drink."

Greenwood smiled. "Neither do I," he said cheerfully. "I sell it to those who do and I have no moral scruples against drinking, but I myself don't drink."

Tom Shanaghy walked back to the street. He was marshal of the town now, and he had no idea what the job paid. Nor did he care.

He stood there, looking around. How did a man go about being a marshal? Where did he start? Shanaghy grinned at his own ignorance. He reflected that one job he had was to fire Drako, but that could wait until the former marshal appeared in town wearing the badge.

That came first. Then he must ride down the country and meet Vince Patterson and talk to him before he arrived in town. And he must, if he could, convince Drako that he must stay out of town until the Patterson outfit was gone.

His thoughts returned to George. George was staying at the same hotel as he was, but where was *she?*

He walked down to the railroad station. The depot had three rooms, all connecting and with doors on both sides. The waiting room, which had four benches, the ticket seller's office (the agent was also the telegrapher and freight agent) and the freight room, where freight was held until shipped or picked up, if incoming. On the train side of the depot there was a rough plank platform, already weathered and gray, about sixty feet long.

Shanaghy stepped into the station and walked to the

window. The agent looked around. He wore a black vest, a white shirt with sleeve-garters, and a green eyeshade. "Somethin' for ya?" he asked. Then he noticed the star.

"Hah? You're the new marshal. What's been done about Drako?"

"Haven't seen him since they gave me this. I am going to tell him when he rides in."

The station agent came to the window and leaned his elbows on the inside counter. "Don't envy you. He's a mean one, and so are those boys of his."

"I've met him, and one of them."

"Got your work cut out for you, and then Patterson comin' up the trail. Boy, I don't envy you! None a-tall!"

"Any railroad detectives working this line?"

"Nah! Why? We've had no trouble."

"If you had a valuable shipment, how would it be handled?"

The agent shrugged. "Same as anything else. It would come in and it would set until picked up. I s'pose if it was very valuable, I'd be wearin' my pistol and they'd be here to pick it up right off."

"You've got a gun then?"

"I have." The agent grinned. "Never fired a shot in my life."

"Then leave it alone," Shanaghy advised. "You'd probably shoot the wrong man."

Shanaghy walked out on the platform and looked down the track. Nothing but twin rails disappearing in the shimmering distance. He doubted if the agent knew about the shipment of money that would be coming in, and to mention it would be merely to start gossip.

He would have to see that men were here to meet the shipment on arrival.

Yet the moment he thought of that, he thought of another aspect. What if they decided to stop the train before it came to town? Chances were, the shipment would be in an express car and guarded only by the agent en route.

For the idea that this was what Rig Barrett guessed would happen had come to Shanaghy only a few hours before. When everybody in town was involved with what might happen when Vince Patterson came to town, the thieves could steal the money brought to pay for the cattle and to pay off the hands.

Barrett might even have had a tip, being the man he was, with connections everywhere.

How many people were involved? And what would be their roles? Plan the job yourself, he suggested to himself, and see how you would do it. You've associated with crooks long enough to know.

The fewer involved, the larger the cut for each, and the less likely they were to be noticed. What if the supposed railroad detective had been a crook? Was the girl involved? And George?

Tom Shanaghy walked up the street to the blacksmith shop and Drako was standing by his horse, waiting. He was wearing a badge.

# Chapter VIII

Tom Shanaghy walked on up and stopped, facing Drako. The man was smiling but he was wary.

"Wearin' a badge, hey? What do you think that will get you?"

Shanaghy had been facing such issues since he first walked off the boat in New York. "I've been appointed town marshal," he said, "and one is all the town needs. I want your badge, Drako."

"You think I'll give it up? Just like that?"

"The authority is not the badge, it is in the vote of the council. They've chosen me Marshal. I want your badge, Drako."

"All right," Drako reached up to unpin the badge, and in that instant Shanaghy knew what the man would do, for it was just what he himself might have done.

Drako unpinned the badge and took it in his left hand and tossed it to him. "Here . . . catch!"

Shanaghy made no move to make the catch. He simply drew his gun, and he was an instant faster . . . Drako had tossed the badge and dropped his hand to his gun, but he was already covered by Shanaghy's pistol.

Drako's hand froze, gripping his gun. Startled, he hesitated, but Shanaghy's thumb was holding his hammer back. And slowly, carefully, Drako released his grip on his gun and moved his hand to the pommel of the saddle. "Smart, hey? We'll see how smart you are when Vince Patterson comes to town."

"He'll be looking for you, not me, and he will know where to find you."

"Maybe."

"You and your boys . . . Come to town whenever you like, only come unarmed."

"Are you crazy?"

76

"That's it. They can hang their pistols in the saloon, but if they wear them on the street I'll throw them in jail."

"What jail? You ain't got no jail!"

"My jail will be that hitching-rail right yonder. I'll shackle them to it and there they'll stay until their fine is paid . . . rain or shine."

Drako stared at him, then turned his horse sharply around and walked him out of town.

Shanaghy picked the badge out of the dust and put it in his pocket. He looked up to see Holstrum watching him. Greenwood was standing in the door of his saloon and Carpenter had stopped work. He ignored the others and walked over to Carpenter. "Be busy for a few days. After that I'll lend you a hand."

"My offer stands. You can buy a piece of my business."

"Maybe . . . later."

Shanaghy went to his room and checked the shotgun. Then, trusting to nothing, he reloaded it with buckshot.

Sitting down on the bed he studied the situation. First he must find out where Patterson might be. Coming up the trail, of course, but where was he now, and moving how fast?

What had he gotten himself into, anyway? There he was, just waiting for the train to take him back to New York, with everything settled in his mind, and now where was he? Marshal of a hick town with all the trouble in the world about to come down on him. What did he know about being a marshal?

Well, someone said, "Set a crook to catch a crook," but he had never been a crook, exactly, although he had known enough of them and had witnessed a lot of their activities.

He looked around the room. Only a bed, a chair and a small table with a lamp on it. In the corner a washstand with a bowl and pitcher. Beside the table was a strip of what passed for a towel, and at the end of the hall a bath.

First thing, he'd better step on down the street and buy some clothes. All he had was what he stood up in, and that was too little. He'd need some shirts, a new suit, and some of those pants they wore around here . . . maybe a hat.

Give up his derby? Not by a damn sight!

That Drako would act. Somehow he was sure. The

man was not about to take this lying down, nor would his boys be willing to do so. Shanaghy knew he could expect trouble from them, and soon.

What bothered him, as it must have bothered the missing Rig Barrett, was the mechanism of the robbery that he believed was to come. How did the crooks expect to handle it, and how many were involved?

He could scarcely believe that the fashionably dressed young woman was involved, and yet why would such a woman be meeting with George? And who was she, anyway?

Tom Shanaghy walked down the street to Holstrum's. There was another man in the store but Holstrum came to wait on the new marshal himself. "You picked yourself a tough job, Marshal, but we'll give you all the support you need."

"Thanks. What I need now is some clothes. I packed light when I came west."

"This on credit?"

Shanaghy smiled. "Cash . . . I always pay cash, Mr. Holstrum. I like to keep the decks clear."

Luckily, he found some shirts. "Most women-folks make shirts for their men," Holstrum explained. "Pendleton buys shirts here and there's a few others."

He bought shirts, underwear, two pairs of pants, a thick leather belt and some boots. He also bought one hundred rounds of .44-pistol ammunition, a Winchester rifle and fifty shotgun shells.

"Expecting a war?" Holstrum asked, curiously.

"No, I'm not. But if one comes, I'll be ready."

"Rig Barrett must figure you could do the job. I never heard of him sending anybody in his place. Didn't know anybody was that close to him."

"Rig kept his personal affairs to himself," Shanaghy replied. "I intend to do the same."

Shanaghy thought for an instant of his past. There had been fistfights, knife fights and gun battles. He could scarcely remember a time when he had not been fighting.

"However," he added, "this is only a precaution. I don't think there will be trouble."

When he had taken his clothes back to the hotel and changed his shirt, Shanaghy came downstairs and went to the restaurant for a late supper.

George was not there, but the young woman was. She

looked up as Shanaghy entered and her eyes fell to the badge. She stared at it, then lifted her eyes to his. He thought he detected a glimmer of anger or impatience.

"How do you do, ma'am?" he removed his derby. "Welcome to our fair city."

She regarded him cooly and then simply turned her head away, ignoring him.

A voice spoke suddenly from behind him on his left, and he looked around quickly. There was a table there, in the corner, and another girl sat there, a younger, perhaps prettier girl. "You're a stranger here yourself, aren't you, Marshal?"

"I am, and saddled with a job before I've got me feet on the ground. But then, by the look of the place, nobody has been here much longer."

The younger girl held out her hand. "I am Jan Pendleton and I want to thank you."

"Me? Wait until I've done something, miss. I am only just marshal."

"You saved Josh Lundy from hanging, and Josh is my very good friend."

"I can't take credit," he said. "They were going to hang me, too, just because I happened to be there. It seemed to me my neck was long enough, without getting it stretched."

"Thank you, nevertheless."

"May I join you?"

"Please do."

He sat where he could see the other woman. She looked annoyed, and that pleased him. He put his derby on the chair beside him and ordered what the restaurant had to offer. There wasn't much variety but he was accustomed to that and had always been a healthy eater.

"Glad you got your horse back," he told her. "Too bad there's so many thieves about. Never could figure out why anybody, man or woman, would take to stealing. They never get as much as they stand to lose.

"You take a woman now. Suppose she was a thief and went to prison? They work 'em almighty hard there, and they've no chance to take care of themselves. And when they come out, they're not only old but they've lost their looks."

The young woman across the room looked up and their eyes met. He smiled and her lips thinned to a hard line.

"Biggest trouble with being a crook," he added, "is the company you have to keep." He paused. "If I saw myself getting involved in such a thing, I'd grab the first train out of town."

Jan looked at him curiously, her eyes flickering to the elegant and composed young woman across the room. She changed the subject.

"Are you going to be with us long, Mr. Shanaghy?"

"It is in my thoughts," he said, "although there be some who hope I'll not."

The cool young woman looked up. "Isn't the life expectancy in your kind of job rather short?"

"It is. Although while I live, the life expectancies of those who break the law will be even less."

He turned from her and began to talk to Jan Pendleton of horses, range, Josh Lundy. "Do you know Mr. Patterson?" he asked suddenly, remembering that her father sometimes bought cattle from him.

"Oh, of course! Uncle Vince is a lovely man! He can be very stern, I suppose, but I've never seen him that way. Whenever he is here he stays with us, and he has such wonderful stories to tell. He gave me my first horse."

"The one that was stolen?"

"The very same. I am glad Josh got it back before Uncle Vince returned, because he would have been furious."

"Seems to me he's already sore at Hank Drako."

"He is." She looked at him seriously. "Mr. Shanaghy, you must not let there be trouble. Father says Uncle Vince may burn the town. He holds all of them responsible for the killing of his brother."

"He'll not burn it," Tom said. "There will be no trouble."

The young woman across the room laughed gently, and Tom Shanaghy felt his face flushing. Before he could speak, however, Jan interrupted. "My father is in town and I am sure he would like to meet you. He will wish to thank you for helping Josh."

Pendleton came in as she was speaking and crossed to the table. After he had talked a bit, Shanaghy said, quite casually, "Mr. Pendleton, you know much of what goes on around here. Do you know of any shipments that have come in during the last couple of days?"

Shanaghy's eyes were on the woman across the room as he spoke, and he saw her fork suddenly stop in mid-air. For just an instant she was absolutely still, then she continued to eat.

"What sort of shipments?"

"I am not quite sure, but I'd be guessing it would be something unusual, or to someone not well known here."

"No . . . I'm afraid not. But then I am not about town very much. What were you thinking of?"

Shanaghy had been talking only to see the face of the woman across the room, for he was but feeling his way. What could it be, after all? What made it important he be off the train?

Or . . . the thought came suddenly, what if it was not some*thing* but some*body?* Suppose there were others hidden on the train who did not wish to chance being seen by a hobo who might climb over the cars looking for a place to hide out?

That was it, that had to be it.

Alfred Pendleton spoke with a decided British accent. Although the Irish had no love for the British, it sounded close enough home to have a pleasant sound. Pendleton asked where Tom was from and Shanaghy replied, "Killarney."

"A lovely place. We vacationed there once."

"And now we are all in Kansas," Jan said.

"And that isn't strange," her father remarked. "There are just two lines of railroad to the west, and most people who come out here stop along one or the other. I am constantly meeting people I knew in England or in the eastern states.

"The fastest development will naturally be along the railroads, and the best opportunities." Pendleton glanced at him. "I suspect you've run into some old friends, haven't you?"

Old friends? What friends did Shanaghy have who might come west? No friends, but what of enemies? Eben Childers was a hater, he had been told, and his men would guess that he took a train to escape them. Finding him would be no great problem. Shanaghy shook his head. "No old friends, and I hope no enemies."

Pendleton talked for a few minutes about the future of Kansas and the way the country was growing and then added, "I think you have chosen wisely, Mr. Shanaghy, in settling here. Carpenter says you are an excellent smith and that you may buy a share of his business."

There it was again. Everybody was taking it for granted that he was here to stay. Shanaghy was remembering John Morrissey and the Bowery, although the memories had been fading away in the warm Kansas sun and the demands of his new job. Then he remembered and looked around. The woman across the room was gone.

"She left a few minutes ago," Jan said, impishly.

"I was wondering who she was and what she was doing here."

"No doubt. She's very attractive, don't you agree?"

"I wasn't thinking of that. But she certainly was . . . is."

"If you are wondering who she is, you could check the register at the hotel," Pendleton suggested.

"She's not registered."

"Not here? But then where . . . ?"

"Exactly. Where else? She's not camping on the plains, and nobody sees her coming and going, although Carpenter did see her riding into town one day."

"You're *very* interested, aren't you?" Jan suggested.

"Yes, ma'am. When there's trouble expected, it is my business to know as much as I can. I don't want anybody to get hurt."

Shanaghy pushed back his chair. "Have you any message for Vince Patterson? I'm riding to meet him."

Pendleton shook his head. "If you're expecting to talk him out of it, forget it. We've tried. He's a stubborn, hardheaded man. But a good man for all of that, and no fool."

"I've got to try."

"You can tell him hello for me," Jan said, "and give him my love."

Well, that word did something to him. Shanaghy wished of a sudden that he was a better man, and he said, "Miss, if that doesn't do it, nothing will."

Then he turned sharply and left, wondering why he was suddenly feeling all hot and embarrassed.

Tomorrow morning he would be riding out, and suddenly he did not want to go anywhere. He just wanted to stay right here.

When the door closed behind him, Pendleton glanced

at his daughter. "An interesting young man," he commented.

"He's nice," she said, "and he's strong . . . very strong."

"Naturally. He's a blacksmith."

"I wasn't thinking of that," she replied. "Perhaps resolute is the word. I don't think he knows what he wants yet, but when he makes up his mind . . . he will get it."

# Chapter IX

The horse Shanaghy rode was a roan, a mustang with a Morgan cross, and the moment he hit the saddle he knew he had a horse. The roan trotted into the street, and the moment he had the room he went to bucking.

Shanaghy, who had ridden all his life, had never tackled anything like this. How he stayed with the horse he never knew, but stay he did. And when finally they loped away he heard a cheer from the few scattered people who had watched.

There had been last-minute advice from Carpenter. The herd would move about twelve miles per day, perhaps less now, as the grass was good and Patterson would want to bring them in fat for the market.

The country, which had appeared flat, proved less so than Shanaghy expected, for there were rolling hills and some deeper ravines. When he was well away from town, he drew up to look around.

As far as the eye could reach there was only grass moving in the wind. These were the fabled buffalo plains, but there were no buffalo now. Far off, he glimpsed a herd of antelope. There was no sound but the wind . . .

For several minutes he sat very still, feeling the wind on his face. The air was fresh, the sky was clear, and somehow the soft wind and the coolness smoothed the troubles from his mind.

Yet . . . the thought came again . . . what of that young woman? Who was she? What was she?

That she was not staying anywhere in town was obvious, and he doubted if she could be living with Hank Drako . . . She simply wasn't the Drakos' type.

That she might live in the town to the west was possible but doubtful, as she seemed too fresh when she rode into town in the morning. True, she had come but twice, but nonetheless she must have somewhere to live that was close by, providing her with a means to keep her clothes pressed and clean.

Where, then?

Puzzling over the question, he rode steadily south, a vast sky above him, a vast sea of grass all about. As he rode, some of the accumulated tension began to dissipate. For the first time in days he began to feel relaxed and rested. He talked to the roan, and the horse twitched his ears, apparently liking the sound of Shanaghy's voice. Shanaghy had always liked horses and he liked this one. Once, sighting a small seep, he turned aside for it and allowed the horse a slow drink while he sat the saddle, studying the country.

He was riding away when he saw the tracks. He knew nothing of tracking, but he could see that at least three horses had passed that way heading for the seep. Turning, he followed the tracks back and found where the riders had dismounted and waited for some time. There were the tracks of the horses and a number of cigarette butts. Then he found the tracks of a fourth rider who had come in from the northeast. Thoughtfully, Shanaghy studied the tracks. Although he knew little or nothing about "reading sign," as the westerners called it, he did know a good deal about horseshoes and the shoeing of horses, and this looked like work Carpenter might have done.

This rider had not dismounted but had remained in the saddle while talking to the others, then had turned around and ridden back along the original trail.

Chances were, it was a casual meeting between some range riders who had stopped for a smoke.

By nightfall, Shanaghy had traveled a distance equal to three days for the herd, and he made camp under some cottonwoods in a little draw where he found the remains of a campfire. He was learning that most places suitable for camps had been used by others before him, but there was water here, some shade, fuel and grass, whatever any traveler might need.

At daybreak he was again on the trail. From what Carpenter and Pendleton had said, he surmised that Patterson would be no more than five or six days' drive from town, and so he rode with his eyes on the horizon to the south, looking for dust or any sign of moving cattle.

It was almost sundown on the second day when he topped out on a small rise and saw them.

They were still miles away to the south, but he could see the long dark line of the moving herd and a few smaller dots that would be outriders. He was still several miles from them when he rode down into a long, shallow valley and saw their chuckwagon, and the thin trail of smoke rising from the campfire. This, then, was where the herd would bed down.

As Shanaghy trotted his horse down the long slope toward the camp, he saw the cook, a man in a once-white apron and battered hat, draw a Winchester from the wagon and lay it across the corner of the tail-gate.

He slowed down as he approached, and walked his horse up to the fire. "I'm looking for the Patterson herd."

The cook, a sour-looking man with a handlebar mustache, noted the badge on Shanaghy's shirt with no approval. "You found it."

"Mind if I wait?"

"Light an' set." Then after a bit of kneading at the dough on the board before him, the cook said, "Where's Rig Barrett?"

"I came in his place."

The cook glanced at him with grim, unfriendly eyes. "They sendin' a boy to do a man's job?"

Tom Shanaghy shoved his derby back on his head. "I been doing man's work since I was twelve," he replied calmly. Then he said, "You must be about the best trail herd cook there is."

The man straightened up. "I do my job." Then he added, "Where'd you get that idea?"

"They tell me Vince Patterson never has anything less than the best."

"Well," the cook's tone was now less surly, "I do what I can. Those are hungry boys, yonder."

"Hope there's enough left for a hungry marshal," Shanaghy said.

He looked up to see two men riding into the hollow. One of them, he immediately guessed, was Vince Patterson. The other was probably his trail boss.

Shanaghy got to his feet. He had decided long ago that he could not fight Patterson and hope to win. One look at the man told him he had decided well. But it had been said that Patterson was a reasonable man, although hardheaded.

"Mr. Patterson?" he said. "I'm Tom Shanaghy, and I need your help."

"Help?" Patterson was surprised. He had expected a warning or a challenge. "What do you mean, you want my help?"

He swung down from the saddle as did the other man. That second man was lean and hard, not a large man but wiry . . . and dangerous. Shanaghy sensed that at once. The man was a fighting man, probably hired for the job.

"When Rig couldn't make it," Shanaghy said, "I had to take over the job for him. But Rig was no damn fool, and he saw right away there was something else involved than a fight between a trail driver and a town."

"What's that mean?"

"Rig figured, and I think the same, that somebody decided to use you."

Patterson stiffened. "Use *me?* I'll be damned if anybody is using me or is going to use me. What kind of talk is that?"

"You're mad at Hank Drako, and rightly so. They heard you were coming up the trail to burn the town where your brother was killed. Now I never put any stock in that, because you're too bright a man to punish a lot of innocent people for what one damn fool did. But there are some others who figured you would do it and that the town would fight . . . which they would, of course."

"So?"

"So these other folks, and I'm not sure who they all are yet, decided that while you and the town were fighting they would steal the money brought in to pay for your herd and to pay off your hands."

Patterson stared at Shanaghy, then turned to the cook. "Fred, give us some coffee, will you?" Then he turned back to Shanaghy. "Sit down. I want to talk to you."

When they were seated, Patterson looked him over cooly. "I don't know you."

"No way you could. Like everybody else out here, I'm a newcomer. The people there in town decided they wanted me to be marshal."

"What happened to Hank Drako?"

"He's around, he and those boys of his." Then he added, "They told me to fire him, and I did."

"You *fired* Hank Drako?"

"I did."

"And he took it?"

"Well, I don't think he liked it very much."

The other man was watching Shanaghy, and Tom knew he was being sized up carefully by a fighting man who knew his business. That part was good. Such men were less apt to make mistakes than a cocky youngster or a would-be tough guy trying to show how bad he was.

"Rig knew something was crossways, Mr. Patterson. He went to Kansas City working on the case. Something happened to Rig there and I had to take over."

Patterson looked at him. "Did Rig feel you were up to the job?"

Shanaghy shrugged. "Well, that's Rig's shotgun over there tied to my saddle."

Somehow or other he had to win this man over to accepting him and his story. He had to get Vince Patterson to stop and think, to help if he would—at least to hold off on whatever he meant to do. And Tom Shanaghy meant to use every artifice he could.

"By the way, Mr. Patterson, I'm carrying a message for you."

"A message? For me?"

"Yes, sir. A very lovely young lady said to say hello and give her love to her Uncle Vince."

The rancher flushed. "That sounds like Jan," his tone was gentler. "Do you know Jan?"

"I've talked to her," Shanaghy said quietly, "I don't know her as well as I'd like to, but I'm quite sure I never will."

Patterson and his trail boss were both looking at Shanaghy and he flushed beet-red. "She's a mighty fine young lady and I'm nothing but an Irish lad who's been given a marshal's job nobody else wanted."

Nobody spoke for a few minutes. The slim man rolled a cigarette and Patterson finally said, "If nobody else wanted the job, why'd you take it?"

"First, because it had to be done. Second, because I thought I could do it. I knew damn well that while I might whip one of your men, or even two or three, I couldn't whip all of you. I was also relying on something Rig said."

"And what was that?"

"He said you were a stubborn, hardheaded man who was also a decent man, and that you were reasonable. He intended to do just what I've done, ride down the trail to talk to you."

"And if I don't listen?"

"I'll protect my town with whatever means I have. If I win, you lose some good men. If you win, you destroy a fine town that's just becoming something. And then you have to drive your herd a hundred and fifty miles across grazed-over ground to another market. And while you and the town are fighting, these other people will steal all that money and we will have aided and abetted them in their crime.

"I know you're an honest man, Mr. Patterson, and no matter how much you hate our town, you don't want to help a bunch of crooks steal the money that was to be paid to you and your men."

The herd was streaming into the valley, and Patterson's trail boss swung into the saddle to help turn them and round them up. Patterson drank his coffee, thinking, and Tom Shanaghy kept his mouth shut.

Finally, Patterson said, "These other people? Who are they?"

"Mr. Patterson," he said slowly, "I'm working on that and right now I just don't know. I think I have three of them spotted, but where they are holed up and just who or how many are involved, I don't know.

"There's a woman involved . . . I think."

"A *woman?*"

"Yes, sir. And the one thing that may be in our favor is that she thinks we are all a pack of fools."

"Maybe we are," Patterson muttered. "Maybe we are."

"Sir? I'm not going to let them get that money. Not one red cent of it."

"You said you wanted my help . . . In what way?"

"This is good grass. The grass around town, and west or east of town, is no way as good as this. I want you to hold off . . . let your cattle fatten while I get this thing worked out. All I need is a couple of days.

"I think," Shanaghy added, "they've got a schedule figured out. I think they know when you're coming in, or about when. I think they have it all set to start, quickly, quietly, efficiently, as soon as you come busting into town to take it apart. While you and the town are busy, they'll get the money and get out . . . Then they'll be gone and we'll be left holding the sack . . .

"If you hold back, three things happen. Your cattle get fatter, their timing is thrown off, and I get a chance to work on the situation before it develops. Personally, I think if their timing is thrown off, something is going to come unglued."

Patterson refilled their cups. "How did you get involved in all this?"

"Well, Drako's son and some others were fixing to hang Josh Lundy. They decided to include me. I persuaded them not to. And, of course, somebody had to take Rig's place."

"Where's Hank Drako now?"

"On his ranch, I expect. Your business with Drako is none of mine. He strikes me as part coyote and part weasel. I think he will kill anything that's helpless or seems so, but if you move against him, don't do it in town."

"You laying down the law?"

"Yes, sir. You lay down the law on your ranch. I do it in town. What you do outside of town is your business and not mine. I wasn't hired to protect the whole state of Kansas, just this town."

Vince Patterson finished his coffee and glanced at his cattle. Some were already lying down, most were still grazing. A few of his men were riding toward the fire. It would be sundown in a little while.

"You staying with us tonight?" Patterson asked.

"With your permission, sir."

Patterson stared at him. "Are you always this respectful?"

Shanaghy grinned. "No, sir. But you're a gentleman, sir, and this is one argument I can't win with my fists or a gun."

Patterson stared for a minute, then chuckled. "All right, damn you, stay the night. I'll sleep on it." He held out his hand. "No promises, mind you, but damn it, Shanaghy, I like you."

# Chapter X

Slowly the hands drifted up to the fire, some of them to bed down, some to catch a quick supper and return to riding herd on the cattle. As they came in they regarded Shanaghy thoughtfully, noticing the badge first, then the derby.

One red-headed cowpuncher looked across the fire at him and said, "That there hat's a temptation. Anybody ever shoot it off you?"

Shanaghy pushed the derby back a little and grinned cheerfully. "Not yet. Maybe that's because they figured I wouldn't know if they were shooting at the derby or me."

He dipped into the stew. "Anyway, it seems a waste of lead. I didn't buy my gun for shooting hats."

He ate in silence for a moment and then said, "The way I figure it, the marshal of a town should be measured by the trouble he keeps clear of town rather than the gunfights he wins. The first thing I did when I took over," he spoke in a low, conversational tone, "was to study the arms situation and the shooters.

"First off I found the town has thirty-seven shotguns, and folks who can use them. We have nine Big Fifty Buffalo guns, two Berdan sharp-shooting rifles, five Winchesters, and seven Spencer fifty-six-calibers. We have fourteen assorted rifles from the Hawken to the Ballard, and every man in town and most of the women have pistols.

"Next thing, I looked over what kind of people we had to do the shooting. Five of the men in town were sharpshooters during the Civil War, one side or the other. Nine others fought in the war. We've got one old mountain-man, and six veterans of Indian battles. There's only two men in town who haven't been in battle, but they're just a frettin' and a fumin' to prove themselves as good as the others.

"Long before I ever saw the place, they figured sometime there might be an Indian raid, so they built the town without any blind spots, front or back. The rifles and shotguns are kept loaded lest there be unexpected trouble, and they are stashed around town easy to hand.

"Most of the folks there want no trouble. They figure outfits like yours will have money to spend, and they're anxious to help. They want to do business with you, the cattle bosses and whoever comes up the trail. They are right friendly folks, but they love their town.

"Me, I'm just a driftin' stranger, and I don't quite see what they like about it but they know. When you boys ride into town I want every one of you to hang up his gun in Greenwood's place."

The redhead laughed, somewhat grimly. "Mister, you've got to be jokin'. I hang up my gun for no man."

"All right," Shanaghy replied cheerfully. "I was just telling you so's you'd know. You see, what worries me isn't you boys at all. It's two or three of the townspeople who are trigger-happy. A couple of those sharpshooters, for example, I've been having trouble convincing them this isn't an all-out war.

"They've agreed to hold their fire and sit tight, but if somebody should in the fullness of his spirits suddenly decide to discharge his piece into the air, that street would turn into a bloodbath.

"All those boys and girls with guns are going to be hunkered down behind log walls or brick walls, and they are going to be shooting into an open street without cover."

Tom Shanaghy shook his head woefully. "Of course, the street's dusty this time of year, and it soaks up blood real fast."

Nobody had anything more to say, and Shanaghy simply finished his meal. After throwing the grounds from his cup, he walked to where his bed-roll lay.

Vince Patterson had sat over at one side and heard it all. He struck a match on the side of his pants, lit a cigar, and approached Shanaghy. "Was that Rig's idea?" he asked mildly.

"Can't blame it on him. Folks there needed a little organization, but they'll go about their business like always unless trouble starts."

"You could be running a bluff."

"Yes, sir. That I could. Be mighty expensive, though, if it was called and I proved to be holdin' the pat hand I've told 'em about.

"Also," Shanaghy added, "I had to have a diversion."

"A diversion?"

"Something to trim the odds, sort of. You've got some loyal hands there. If trouble started in town and then something happened to your herd, I figure about half your men would cut and run to protect the cows."

"What could go wrong with my herd?"

Shanaghy shrugged. "Well, a few days ago some Kiowas showed up. Least that's what the old-timers said they were. I don't know one Indian from another.

"Well, these Kiowas had been raiding Pawnees up the country a bit, they caught the short end of the stick, and they were sore.

"We fed 'em, and I sort of suggested they stay around and keep out of sight. I also suggested that it might be worth a bunch of presents if they sort of listened for gunfire."

Patterson was looking at him. "Gunfire?"

"Uh-huh. If they heard gunfire from town, they were to stampede your herd."

Patterson swore.

"Stampede 'em, and scatter them all over the prairie."

Patterson swore again, and then he said, "But we have you, Marshal. What about that?"

"You would lose a man or two taking me, Mr. Patterson, but it would change nothing. You see, the way that plan of mine is set up, it works without anybody saying anything. They don't need me at all now.

"Things been pretty dull around town lately. No fights to speak of, and the boys are kind of restless, kind of keyed up, if you know what I mean."

"You seem to have thought of everything."

"I've tried. You see, I've heard your boys ride for the brand. Well, that town is my brand. They hired me to do a job, and I'm doing it the best way I know how."

Later, Shanaghy lay in his blankets staring up at the stars. He had lied, of course. His plans were not nearly so thorough as he had implied. Nonetheless, they were good plans and he planned to put them into execution as soon as he got back . . . *if* he got back.

If he avoided trouble and saved some lives with his

stories, all would be well. At least he had offered a little doubt, and nobody wanted to get shot down in the street. If what he had said was not true, it was all possible, and they could not know whether he was telling the truth or not.

When he heard stirring around the camp he got up. It was not yet four o'clock in the morning, he noticed by his big silver watch, but the camp was coming alive. He crawled out of bed, put on his derby and then got into his pants and boots.

Nobody was paying any attention to him, and he went to the fire for his grub along with the others.

Patterson was there. He glanced at Shanaghy, gave a short nod and went on eating.

The air was clear and cool. There was a smell of dust and cattle on the air, and off to one side a cowpuncher was letting his bronc buck the kinks out of his system. Nobody was talking until he went to get coffee and Red picked up the pot and filled his cup for him.

Red grinned at him. "You spin a good yarn, Marshal, but, you know, we didn't figure any of it was worth throwin' a loop over."

"I can carve it on your headstone," Shanaghy said.

"What?"

" 'He asked to be showed; we showed him.' "

"Hey," Red said, "that ain't bad! I've seen men buried with less."

"To tell you the truth, Red," Shanaghy said, "I'd rather buy you a drink than shoot you."

"Well, now," Red said cheerfully, "I'll remember that, Marshal. How many do you figure to set up for?"

"Hell," Shanaghy said, "I'll buy a drink for the whole crew. You're a good bunch of lads."

He finished his coffee. "Besides, you've got a good cook."

He saddled up. As he was tightening his cinch, Vince Patterson walked over. "Don't expect us for about four or five days, Marshal. And if you need any help with those hold-up people, you let us know. We'll ride with you."

Shanaghy held out his hand. "Rig sure had you figured. He said you were a decent and a reasonable man."

They shook hands. "Shanaghy," Patterson said, "I think Jan Pendleton is the finest girl I know, but she could do a whole lot worse than you."

Tom Shanaghy flushed. "Mr. Patterson," he said, "don't you even think that. I'm not the man for her, and I know she's given no thought to me. Why, she's only seen me once."

"I married my wife the second time I saw her," Patterson said, "and we've got twenty years of happiness behind us."

Tom Shanaghy turned his horse and rode away.

He had gone only two horse-lengths when Patterson called after him. "What about Hank Drako?"

"Hank's going to be hunting me, he and his boys. If they find me, you've got no problem. If you boys find them you can have them, just so it's out of town."

He rode hard. There were things he had to do, and time was short, and he did not think of Jan Pendleton. At least, he tried not to.

The town lay quiet in the late afternoon sun when Shanaghy rode into the street. He took his horse to Carpenter's stable and stripped off the gear. He gave the roan a good rubdown, thinking all the while, then took his saddle-bags and walked over to the blacksmith shop.

Carpenter looked up. "Holstrum was by. Wanted to know where you were."

"Drako been around?"

"Not hide nor hair." Carpenter put down his hammer. "Had it for today." He took off his leather apron. "Oh, by the way! That young woman you're interested in. She came by. Wanted a horse shod . . . today."

"You do it?"

"Uh-huh. A different horse, too. Sometimes I wonder about eastern folks. Seem to think horses all look alike."

"Pendleton been around?"

"No, but his son was in. He was asking for you."

Shanaghy was not concerned about young Pendleton. His thoughts were on the robbery . . . Or was he simply seeing ghosts? What did he have, after all, but a lot of suspicions?

A strange girl in town for no apparent reason, who kept to herself. In other words, she was simply minding her own business.

Her odd association with a man who looked like a tinhorn gambler, and the puzzle about where she lived.

A man on a train who Shanaghy had believed to be a railroad detective and who apparently was not.

Rig Barrett's suspicions that something was in the wind, which Shanaghy was inclined to trust.

And the fact that somebody seemed to have taken pains to eliminate Rig before he could arrive in town.

And the knowledge that a lot of money, probably a quarter of a million in gold and bills, would be arriving on the train someday soon.

Who knew of that? Almost everybody in town who did not actually know could surmise. So could a lot of others. After all, there had to be money on hand. Such a town would not ordinarily have so much, so it would have to be brought in.

That man on the train now . . . Now that Shanaghy considered it, that man had not seemed western. Well, why should he? Neither was he, Tom Shanaghy.

The trouble with Vince seemed to have been averted, but nobody knew that but him. He decided nobody must know, not if he could help it.

He turned toward the hotel and halted suddenly. A man was riding toward him on a buckskin horse.

"Howdy!" It was Josh Lundy. "Remember me?"

"I do."

"Figured you might need some help. My boss give me a few days off and I thought I'd ride in to see if you needed a hand."

"You could get killed."

"You didn't seem to pay much mind down by the creek that day."

"I was saving my own hide."

"No matter."

Shanaghy liked the cowhand and remembered Rig's estimate of him. The man was seasoned, tough, and had local experience, knowing local people whom Shanaghy did not. "Let's get over to Greenwood's and I'll buy you a beer," he suggested.

From where they sat, as Shanaghy had correctly remembered, they could look down the street. Besides, it was quiet here and they could talk.

"Watch yourself." Greenwood walked over to give the warning. "There's talk that Drako and his boys are coming into town after you."

He had started away when Shanaghy said, "Who told you that?"

"Holstrum . . . I guess somebody said something about it over at the store."

They sipped their beers and slowly, carefully, Shanaghy told Josh Lundy of the suspected plan to seize the money shipment.

His thoughts returned to the hoofprints by the seep. "Anybody running cattle in south of here?" He explained his interest.

"Drifters, more than likely. There's a lot of odd characters stop by Drako's place." Lundy paused. "Four of them, you say?"

"It looked to me like somebody brought them a message. He didn't get off his horse, just talked awhile and left."

"Mostly guesswork, Marshal."

Suddenly Lundy said, "Is that the girl you've been talking about, Marshal?"

It was . . . She came riding up the street, then dismounted in front of the café.

Shanaghy got to his feet. "Josh, I'm going to have a talk with her. Right now."

# Chapter XI

It was cool and quiet in the restaurant and at this hour it was empty, something she had no doubt counted upon. When Shanaghy entered she looked up, a flash of annoyance crossing her face.

After crossing to her table, he said, "Mind if I sit down?"

She looked up. Beautiful, she undoubtedly was, but her features might have been cut from marble. "I do, indeed. I wish to be alone."

"I am sorry, ma'am, but I have some questions."

"And I have no answers. Must I call the manager?"

"If you like."

She looked at him with contempt. "If you wish to take advantage of your authority, ask what questions you will. I shall decide whether or not to reply."

"Fair enough. Mind telling me how long you've been here?"

"In this town? Slightly over a week."

"What's your purpose here?"

Her expression was one of exasperated patience. "I am looking for ranch property. My father was unable to come, and we share our financial interests. We are looking for good grass and a source of permanent water."

Shanaghy felt like a fool. Of course, what could be more likely? "Found anything that suits you?"

"No . . . There are two possibilities, that is all. Now, is there anything more?"

"Do you expect to be here long?"

She put her cup down sharply. "Marshal, or whatever you are called, I have told you why I was here, and I am on legitimate business. I am not the sort of woman who expects to be badgered by every small-town officer with an exaggerated sense of his own importance. Unless you

walk. He got up, leaving money on the table, and went outside.

Who was the rider? Had he actually spoken to George? Had the girl been angry because it all happened while he, Shanaghy, was watching?

Was the rider a messenger? If so, from whom? Did Patterson know he had come?

Shanaghy hesitated, then turned toward Greenwood's. No guns were to be worn in town, he had said. Well, that meant now.

Or was this man merely bait for a trap? Perhaps today was the day they meant to eliminate *him*. Tom Shanaghy had served too long with Morrissey not to suspect such things.

If this man was bait, there would be others around. They would not be likely to trust such a job to one man alone, unless he was very, very good.

Even then they would have someone else. They would want some insurance. Which meant another marksman.

Would that be George?

For several minutes Shanaghy sat still, thinking it over. Wherever the girl had gone it was not to the street, for she had not appeared there. He finished his coffee and went back through the kitchen and out the back door—but only after a careful glance up and down to see if anyone lurked there.

At the corner of a building, he hesitated, looking around it toward the saloon. From there, he had a good view of the swinging doors. This rider was from Patterson's outfit and he had issued his ultimatum to them . . . no guns in town. Now this man had ridden in wearing his guns . . . Was it a test? A direct challenge?

Or maybe the man had gone to the saloon to hang up his guns?

If not, the challenge must be met, and he would meet it now.

From inside the saloon the patrons could see up and down the street, but approaching the building indirectly, Shanaghy could be crossing the street before they saw him. He was in the middle of the street and walking fast before he glimpsed the two horses tied in the alleyway beside Holstrum's store, and then he was going up the steps and into the saloon.

Two strangers sat at a table on the right side of the

saloon. The Patterson rider was at the bar. Greenwood looked up and directly at him, but he said nothing.

Shanaghy walked to the bar. "Sorry, cowboy," he said, smiling, "while you're in town you will have to hang up the guns. Mr. Greenwood will take them for you."

"Hang up my guns?" the cowhand took a half-step back. "You want my guns, you got to take them!"

The man was ready, and so were the other two. "Oh, well," Shanaghy replied cheerfully, "if you feel that way about it." He turned away and to the bar, as if no longer caring.

Frustrated in his attempt to start a fight, the cowhand let his hands fall away from his guns, and Shanaghy hit him.

It was a smashing back-hand blow to the mouth, yet no sooner had the blow struck than Shanaghy's hand dropped to the cowhand's shoulder and grabbed him by the collar. Shanaghy jerked the man into a wicked left hook to the belly. Flipping the man around with his back to Shanaghy, the marshal flipped his guns from the twin holsters, covering the two men at the table.

"Get up!" he spoke sharply, but cooly. "Get up and unfasten your gunbelts!"

"Look here! You got no call to—!"

"Now," Shanaghy shoved the gasping cowboy toward them, rearing back both hammers. The clicks of the cocking hammers were loud in the room.

"All right," the shorter man said, "looks like you got—"

He drew, and Tom Shanaghy shot him through the tobacco tag hanging from his shirt pocket. The man went down, and the left-handed gun was on the other.

His face yellow and sick-looking the second man slowly, carefully, lifted his hands.

"Put 'em down," Shanaghy said, "and let go your gunbelt. If you feel lucky, you just play the fool like your partner did."

He shoved the cowhand he had grabbed over to the table. The cowhand was grasping his side, a pained expression on his face. "Damn you!" he said. "You busted a rib!"

"Only one? That punch is usually good for three. My best day it was five, but he was coming at me."

Without turning his head, he spoke to Greenwood.

"See what you can do for that man, will you? He's hurt but he's not dead."

He gestured with a gun, shoving the other into his waistband. "Court ain't in session," he said, "so I'll handle it. Fifty dollars or fifty days."

"Hell, who's got that much money?"

"If you've got a friend who has," Shanaghy said cheerfully, "you'd better get word to him. Start walking now . . . outside."

The hitching rail in front of the smithy was built with posts of good size set deep in the earth, and the rail itself was of oak, notched into the posts and spiked in place. He handcuffed each man to the rail by one wrist.

"How long you goin' to leave us here?"

Shanaghy did not smile. "Fifty days, unless you can come up with the fine."

"Fifty days? You're crazy! What if it rains?"

"Well," Shanaghy said, "the overhang will protect you if the rain comes from thataway. Otherwise, I'd say you're liable to get wet. The same thing goes for the sun."

Shanaghy pushed his derby back on his head. "You boys came in here asking for it. Maybe the man who sent you will put up your fines." He grinned suddenly. "But I've a notion he'll just let you rot. You're no good to him any more."

"When I get loose—!"

Shanaghy shook his head reprovingly. "That's the feelin' that got you into trouble. My advice is to just pull your freight and get out of here."

"Where'd a man who wears a derby learn to use a gun like that?"

Shanaghy smiled. "I had a good teacher, and a lot of time to practice."

He went back to Greenwood's. The place was empty and Greenwood was mopping the floor. "How is he?"

Greenwood shrugged. "If he's lucky, he'll live. If your bullet had been an inch or two lower, he'd never have made it to the doctor."

Greenwood took his mop and bucket to the back room and returned, drying his hands. "You don't waste around much, do you?"

"I do not. At such a time a man can only do what he must."

Shanaghy drank part of a beer and then remembered the horses. Leaving his beer on the bar, he went out quickly and hurried down the street. He rounded the corner into the alley beside Holstrum's store and pulled up.

The horses were gone . . .

# Chapter XII

Shanaghy stood for an instant, realizing that the horses might have belonged to someone other than the men in the saloon. But if such was the case, who did they belong to?

He glanced down at the tracks. One resembled a track seen at the seep where the unknown riders had met.

Turning, he walked back up the street, but as he went, he was thinking. If those horses had belonged to the men in the saloon, they were still in town . . . Nobody had ridden out, for in this wide-open country, except at night, it was impossible to enter or leave town without being seen.

He returned to Greenwood's. "Know any of those men?" he asked the saloon-keeper.

Greenwood shrugged. "They're strangers, Tom. The minute they walked in I had them pegged for trouble. A man in my business has to know."

"Mine, too."

"You acted like you knew what to do!"

Shanaghy shrugged. "I broke up fights and bounced tough guys out of Bowery saloons when I was sixteen. I've been through that a couple of hundred times."

"With guns?"

"Sometimes. More than likely slung-shots, billies or chivs . . . knives, I mean. You take the mean one first . . . Then the others lose their stomach for it.

"That one," he added, "he was going to start trouble, and the others were going to shoot me."

"Rig Barrett couldn't have done it better."

Shanaghy looked at Greenwood. "No? Well, maybe. He'd more than likely have it all figured out now and know who the front man was."

"You believe there is one?"

"Look . . . Some of these boys came in from out of town. This job was planned out of town. Rig knew that. So how did they know about it? Either somebody tipped them off or they had a tip from the place that will supply the money."

"I wish I could have seen those horses," Greenwood mused.

"Seen 'em? Why?"

"I'd know if they were from around here. Hell, Tom, every western man knows horses and he doesn't forget them."

Suddenly, Shanaghy swore. "Damn! That must've been what Carpenter meant!"

"Meant? What was that?"

"Awhile back he made some comment to the effect that somebody didn't realize that horses could be remembered, or something like that. I think he recognized the horse that girl was riding."

"You surely don't think she's involved? That girl's a lady."

Shanaghy shrugged. "Anybody can want money, and I've seen some pretty cold-blooded ladies. I've seen them at cockfights and dogfights, real blue-stockings, and enjoying every minute of it."

He walked out again on the street. Right now he was wishing he had a friend, any kind of a friend. He was wishing he could talk to McCarthy or Old Smoke Morrissey, or that old-timer who taught him to use a six-shooter. He needed somebody he could talk to . . . and he had no idea whether Greenwood could be trusted or not.

He thought of Holstrum, but the storekeeper was a quiet, phlegmatic sort not likely to be of any help.

Carpenter . . . ? He turned toward the smithy, suddenly aware that he had heard no ringing of the hammer for some time.

He walked more swiftly as he neared the smithy, and suddenly saw a woman standing in the entrance, shading her eyes with her hand as she looked his way.

"Are you Tom?" she said as he walked up. "I'm Mrs. Carpenter."

"I was looking for your husband."

"So was I. I brought his lunch and he wasn't here. The forge is almost cold. I can't imagine—"

"In this town? Where could a man go?"

"He might be at Greenwood's. He said something to me this morning about having a talk with him."

She paused. "Marshal? Would you go there for me? A lady can't go into such places."

"He's not at Greenwood's. I've just come from there."

"I'm frightened, Marshal. It isn't like him. He's . . . he's a very meticulous man . . . about everything. If he had been going anywhere he would have told me."

"Ma'am? Did he talk any about horses? I mean, did he say anything about a horse he'd recognized lately?"

"No . . . not that I can recall. He's been preoccupied, and that's unlike him. I think he has been worried."

"So have we all, ma'am. So have we all."

Shanaghy paused, then continued: "Ma'am?" She was a pleasant-looking, attractive woman. Had someone asked her what she was, she would have said, "housewife," and been proud of it. "Ma'am? I can use your help.

"You know the people in this town. I am still a stranger. Anyway, sometimes women are more perceptive about people than men are. Something's going on here. I think somebody is planning to steal the money that's being brought into town to pay for cattle and to pay off the drivers. Mostly it will be outside people, but I think somebody right here in town is in on it, and may have started the whole thing.

"There aren't many secrets in a town of this size, and I want you to think about it. Meanwhile, I'll have a look for your husband. If he comes back, let Greenwood know."

"Do you trust him? He's a saloon-keeper."

"I trust no one. Not even you. But I *think* he's an honest man."

"Enough money, that much money, would tempt many an honest man. My husband worked very hard this past year, and he has made just over seven hundred dollars. That's pretty good. I doubt if either Mr. Greenwood or Mr. Holstrum has done any better, so think of what two hundred and fifty thousand dollars represents."

"Ma'am, I've known crooks most of my life, but the honest men I knew . . . well, I don't think some of them would sell out at any price. I don't believe your husband would."

She started to turn away, then hesitated. "Marshal?

Who is that young woman who is staying at the hotel? The very attractive one we see riding about?"

"She says she's looking at land, that she and her father are prospective buyers." He paused. "But she isn't staying at the hotel."

"Not at the hotel? Then where—?"

"I've no idea, ma'am. Yet you've seen her. She's always neat, never dusty, her clothes always fresh and clean. She's not camping out, ma'am."

Holstrum was behind the counter of his store. He peered at Shanaghy over his glasses and smiled. "Ah? You come to my little store, Marshal? What can I do for you?"

"I'm looking for Carpenter."

"Carpenter, is it? Ah, no. Not today, I think." He waved a hand. "But who knows? We see each other often, one day is like the next. He is not at his shop?"

Shanaghy shook his head. He liked the store, and the pleasant smells of dry goods, slabs of bacon, fresh-cut chewing tobacco, new leather from the saddles and bridles, and coffee from the coffee-grinder.

"Sometimes, Marshal, I think you worry too much. When the men of Patterson comes you can talk. Maybe he will listen to you."

"Maybe." He looked out of the window at the empty street. A hatful of breeze caught at the dust and swirled it, then dropped it reluctantly. He went to the huge circular cheese under glass and lifted it, slicing off an edge for himself, then he strolled back to the counter.

"Maybe I should go back to New York," he muttered. "Since coming here I've been thinking of other things than myself. I'm growing soft."

"It is a small place here," Holstrum agreed. "We have not much to offer."

"Where were you from, Holstrum? Another small town?"

"A farm," the older man said. "On a farm I was born. On a farm I lived. There was work, much work. Morning, noon and night, there was work. Always, I think of other places, better places than the farm. I think of women, too, of soft, warm, beautiful women mit perfume. On the farm I see no such women. My mama, she is gone before I know more than her face, and we are all men. My father, he drives us. Always it is work."

"So you came west?"

"I work on a boat on the canal. Then I come to Chicago, where I work. I save a little. I see always people with much. I envy them. I go where they go and stand outside and look in on them.

"They are rich people. Their women are soft and warm, and when they passed me going from their carriages, I smell their perfume. So I say, someday . . ."

He broke off. "A boy's foolishness, that's what it was. Now I have good business. Soon I shall be rich man."

"What happened to the farm? And your brothers who stayed?"

Holstrum shrugged. "My father is dead. The farm is now only one of five farms. They have done well, my brothers. One also owns a store. One has a bank."

Shanaghy finished the cheese. "You might have been a banker had you stayed, but you wouldn't have seen all this." He waved a hand.

Holstrum stared at him over his glasses. "I do not like all this. Sometime I will have a big business in a big town . . . You'll see."

Shanaghy grinned. "And maybe the woman with the perfume . . . or have you found her already?"

Holstrum lowered his head and stared at the marshal over his glasses. For a moment he peered at Shanaghy, then shook his head. "One time I think I meet such a woman. She wished to go to a fine place so I dress in my new black suit and take her there. We ate and we talked, but I do not know what she says . . . many words of things of which I know nothing." He paused. "I never see her again. And the meal," he added, "it cost me all I would earn in one week. For *one* meal.

"Someday," he added, "it will not be so! I shall eat many such meals, and I shall not think of cost! I will know many such women, and they will not think small of me."

"You think she did?"

"I never see her again. When I go to ask they say she is not at home, or is not 'receiving.' "

"Tough," Shanaghy said. "That could happen to anyone." He was thinking of Jan Pendleton. What a fool Holstrum was! But he wouldn't be. Not by a damned sight. He wasn't going to make a fool of himself.

By suppertime they all knew Carpenter was gone. None of his horses were missing. His saddle was in the barn.

His pistol, rifle and shotgun were all in place. Yet Carpenter was nowhere around.

The judge was in the restaurant when Shanaghy came in. He remembered him from that first night when some man had come in to tell the judge that something must have happened to Rig Barrett. The judge nodded when he saw Shanaghy.

He held out his hand. "Marshal? I am Judge McBane. Judge by courtesy, that is. Once, back in Illinois, I was a judge. Out here I am merely another lawyer, trying to make a living."

"We need a judge, and we need a court. The nearest one is miles away."

"You may be right. Sometimes I think the fewer laws the better. We are an orderly people, we Americans, although others do not think of us so."

He was a short, heavy-set man with a bulging vest, a heavy watch-chain with a gold nugget and an elk's tooth suspended from it, and a thick mustache that covered his upper lip and most of his mouth. "I understand our smith has disappeared?"

"Well . . . he doesn't seem to be around. But there are no horses missing that we've heard of, and all his are in the corral."

The judge led the way to a table, seated himself and brushed his mustache with the back of his forefinger, first the right side, then the left.

"He was in to see me," the judge commented casually, his eyes roaming the room. "Said the horses of those men you have chained down in the street had disappeared."

"They have."

Judge McBane turned his slightly bulging eyes back to Shanaghy. "Seems to me," he suggested, speaking quietly, "that a marshal looking for a missing man could go through every stable in town. If he didn't find Carpenter he might find those horses. Their brands might tell him something."

Shanaghy flushed. "Of course!" He shook his head ruefully. "I'm new at this business, Judge, but why couldn't I think of what's so obvious?"

"I do it all the time," the judge replied cheerfully.

Shanaghy got up suddenly. "Judge? If I may be excused—?"

Later, he thought, How did I remember to say that?

He had not realized there were so many stables in the town, but where horses are used there must be places in which to keep them.

In the ninth stable, near an abandoned corral, both by the smell and by struck matches, Shanaghy found fresh manure and places where the horses had stood. They were gone now.

He was turning away when he saw the boot-toe. It was barely showing above the hay in the long manger—hay with which a body had obviously been hastily covered.

Even before he brushed away the hay, Tom Shanaghy knew.

It was Carpenter.

# Chapter XIII

He had been struck over the head, then stabbed at least three times. The blow over the head seemed to have come from behind.

Shanaghy thought of Mrs. Carpenter and swore softly, bitterly. He would have to tell her. It was something that must be done, and now.

Yet first, he must look around. Whoever had killed Carpenter had come here with him, or had come up behind him. It was unlikely that Carpenter had been killed elsewhere and brought here. Undoubtedly he had found the horses and been killed at that moment.

Why kill him for seeing the horses unless the horses pointed to someone? Yet from what he had gathered there were few local brands. There were but a few local people who ran cattle, and the farmers did not have any but a few milk cows which they kept up or picketed on grass so they could not stray.

Shanaghy straightened up and stood very still, thinking. He had started to strike another match when he heard a faint stirring . . . Was it outside? Or inside?

Careful to make no sound, he eased himself back into the stall and squatted on his heels.

The double doors of the stable stood open. Along one side was a row of four stalls, divided one from another simply by horizontal poles and floor-to-roof posts. The manger was simply a long trough that extended through all four stalls.

On the opposite side there was simply the wall. Nails had been driven into the boards on which to hang odd bits of old harness, links of chain, and whatever had been lying around loose. Near that wall was a wooden bucket and a pitchfork. On the ledge formed by a two-by-four that ran the length of the side between supporting posts, there had been a currycomb, a brush and some heavy shears.

At the back of the barn was a window. Here and there cracks allowed a glimpse of the lights of the town. The nearest building was about fifty yards off, the pole corral on the side away from the town.

Somebody had either come here with Carpenter or had followed him here. Perhaps had lain in wait for him. And Carpenter was dead.

Again, a faint stirring. Shanaghy cleared the thong from the hammer of his six-shooter. He heard a faint creak and looked up. One of the big barn doors was slowly swinging shut!

He started to rise . . . Was it a trap? Or just the wind?

He was in the fourth and last stall. He got up suddenly and started for the door. As he did so it swung shut and he heard a latch drop into place.

Rushing to the door, he pushed against it, but the door held firm. He knew the hasp on the door couldn't be very strong. He stepped back to lunge against it, hesitated, for fear of a shot, then threw himself at the barrier.

The door was immovable. Something was wedged against it from the outside. He turned quickly toward the window . . . It was too small!

For an instant Shanaghy stood perfectly still. This was stupid! What in the world could be the reason? Nobody could be kept locked up like this for long. He would get out on his own, or, when morning came and people began moving about, he could call out . . .

If he was alive.

Realization came to him one instant before he smelled the smoke.

*Fire!*

Destroying not only him, but Carpenter's body, as well —Carpenter's body with its telltale wounds.

Shanaghy was no fool to waste time in charging about or battering at walls. The closest buildings were stores, empty at night. The feeble sounds he could make, unless he started shooting, would attract no attention, and even the shots might be passed off as some drunk celebrating a little.

The smoke was coming through cracks from the north side of the barn, the side away from the town, and from the smell it was hay burning. Hay would create the most smoke, and might smoulder for some time before growing into flame, but it was smoke that killed most people in fires. Shanaghy knew that from the firemen working Morrissey's volunteer companies in New York.

He had to get out, and he had to get Carpenter's body out. He'd never get the doors battered down in time.

The smoke was getting thicker. As he ran to Carpenter's body, he started coughing. He lifted the smaller man from the manger . . . to the back of the barn.

The loft . . . the small loft where hay was stored for use during bad weather! There was a simple ladder of crosspieces nailed to a post that gave access to the loft.

Higher up, the smoke would be worse. No matter. It was the only way. Lifting Carpenter's body, Shanaghy slung it over his shoulder. Holding the body in place, he grasped the post itself with his free hand and climbed.

Five steps. He dumped the body on the little hay that remained. Then, coughing and grasping, he reached for the roof.

It was made of poles with a crude thatch of branches and straw. Almost unable to breathe, his eyes smarting from the smoke, he clawed at the poles with his bare hands. He ripped and he tore. He got hold of a branch and broke it free. Dust and dirt cascaded over him. He tore at the thatch, coughing with great, lung-tearing gasps. Suddenly, his hand went through and fresh air flooded around him. Below him, he heard the crackle of flames from inside the barn.

After ripping branches away, he grasped a pole and broke it by sheer brute strength. More dust and straw tumbled through upon him, but there was more fresh air, too.

Stooping, he grabbed Carpenter's body by the collar and crawled through the hole onto the roof. Flames were leaping up behind him. None were yet visible outside, although there was considerable smoke.

After reaching the edge of the barn, he dropped the body and leaped down himself, falling quickly to one side, gun in hand.

Nothing . . . the would-be killer was gone, fearful of being seen close to the burning barn.

Tom Shanaghy gathered Carpenter's body in his arms and walked slowly away. Behind him the barn exploded into flame, and he heard shouts and yells from the town.

The Carpenter home was but a hundred yards or so away, and he walked toward it.

She was standing on the step, looking toward the fire, and she saw him coming. He saw the white of her wrapper when she stepped away from the door and came toward him, walking slowly.

"Marshal? Mr. Shanaghy? Is it him?"

"Yes, ma'am. He was murdered, ma'am."

"Marshal, would you bring him in, please?" Then she paused. "What is happening, Marshal?"

"I found his body, but they locked me in the stable and set it afire."

She indicated a bed and he placed the body there, gently. "Ma'am? They'd left him in the manger, covered with hay, but the worst of this is from bringing him through the roof."

"Even then, with the fire, you took time to bring him out? Marshal, I—"

"Ma'am, forget it. And don't worry. I'll find who did it. I'll find them if it's the last thing I ever do."

Men had crowded around the fire, watching to keep it from spreading, although the building was isolated. Shanaghy glanced toward them and went on to the street again, pausing there a moment to brush the dust from his derby.

There were still a few horses along the street and there was one rig . . . A man was untying the horses and he turned at Shanaghy's footsteps. It was Pendleton.

Shanaghy paused. "Leaving town, Mr. Pendleton? You aren't staying for the fire?"

"I have seen a fire, Marshal." The Englishman turned toward him. "What has happened?"

"Carpenter has been murdered. I had just found the body when somebody set fire to the barn. An attempt, I presume, to destroy both me and the evidence."

"But you got out? And the body?"

"I brought it with me. Is Jan with you?"

"At this hour?"

"I was hoping she was. Somebody . . . a woman, I think, should be with Mrs. Carpenter. I could think of no one better than Jan."

"I'll bring her in. But there's Mrs. Murphy, too, over at the boardinghouse."

Puzzled, Shanaghy watched Pendleton drive away. It was late, almost midnight, in fact, and not a likely hour for anybody to be out. Western towns were not like New York. Here, people arose at daybreak or before and worked the day through. By night they were ready for bed, and sleep.

Shanaghy watched the receding back of the buckboard and then walked across to the hotel.

Carpenter was dead and an attempt had been made to kill him, so it was no longer fun- and party-time. Also, somebody had either been watching the barn or trailing him. More likely the latter.

From his room in the hotel, Shanaghy looked down into the street. He had no light burning and offered no target, yet he himself could see into the street. He was puzzled.

He had always been wary of being followed. This caution had developed from his days around the Five Points, for the area had been a hangout for thugs. Even the children would rob a man, setting on him in gangs and tripping him up or pulling him down. Shanaghy was as sure as a man could be that he had not been followed. Yet he had been observed.

Somebody, or several somebodies, was taking time out from whatever else they were doing to watch him . . . which meant they were worried.

First they had tried to have him killed in Greenwood's, and second, in the burning barn. What next? That there would be another attempt, and that it would be soon, he knew.

He put his derby on the dressing table, took off his boots, and sat down on the edge of the bed.

What actually did he have? He believed an attempt was to be made to steal the money, which was due in the day after tomorrow by the latest reports.

He believed the mysterious young woman was involved. He believed the supposed railroad detective who had put him off the train was also involved.

Whoever was in on the action had a local base, and sources of local information.

That person, or persons, had hidden the horses, had attempted to kill him.

He thought of the men down there in the street. He had taken food to them, and water. What disturbed him was that they seemed less worried by their captivity than expected.

Escape would not be easy. The posts were deeply sunk and the railing was thick, strong, well-seasoned wood. The sound of a saw or an ax would be heard all over town. Digging the posts out of the ground would be a formidable job.

Had they received some promise they would be taken care of?

Irritably, he got up and paced the floor. In just a matter of hours, the money would be arriving. If Vince Patterson did not come in with his cattle and his riders, the robbers would have planned some other diversion. As quietly as possible, he moved his bed closer to the window, put two pillows behind him and sat up, looking out at the street. From where he sat he could see the two men chained to the hitching-rail. Both seemed to be asleep, and the street was empty.

By now the plotters might have discovered that Patterson was not to make his move. In any event, he must think that way and not blind himself to whatever else might happen.

Suddenly, he sat up. One of the men at the hitching-rail had lifted his head and was peering intently across the street toward a place hidden from Shanaghy's view.

Shanaghy got up, pulled on his boots and slipped into his coat. After donning his derby, he went quietly down the stairs into the deserted lobby. A faint light glowed over the desk but all else was dark. He moved to the wide window where, standing near the pillar, he had a good view up and down the street.

Suddenly he saw the hand of one of the chained men shoot up as if to catch something, then saw him clawing in the dust to get hold of it.

Shanaghy wheeled. Moving swiftly, he went down the hall. At the back door he paused, then eased the door open, and slipped out into the darkness. As he did so a figure emerged from between the buildings and moved away from him.

There was no chance for identification, not even a glimpse of more than the shadowy figure. Shanaghy started after him, running as softly as possible on the sandy earth.

Some sound must have reached the figure ahead, for Shanaghy caught a glimpse of a startled white face. Then the figure broke into a run, disappearing around a corner.

Shanaghy pulled up at the corner, expecting a trap. Then he heard a pound of hoofs and he rushed from between the buildings to catch the merest suggestion of movement and the sound of retreating hoof-beats.

He swore, then spat. The luck of him! Another step or two faster and he might have caught at least a glimpse.

Wearily, he walked back to the hotel and went to bed. He was not especially interested in what had been thrown. He was pretty certain what it had been . . . a lock pick, he was sure. At this point he didn't care, for if the three escaped it would be all the less to watch out for when the showdown came.

He awakened in the cold light of dawn unrested, worried and sure that things were completely out of control.

All hell was about to break loose, and he did not know where or from who or just how.

When he had eaten breakfast he went from place to place, trying to complete setting up the organization he had told Patterson was already in existence. There was some grumbling, but there was also some eagerness. Things had been quiet in town and some of the townsfolk were ready for action, any kind of action.

Work had piled up at the blacksmith shop. After taking off his coat and shirt he put on a leather apron and went to work. He always thought better when his hands were busy, anyway. Physical labor seemed to open all the channels of his mind.

He completed an order for andirons, made two sets of hinges and put shoes on two horses. It was when he was paring down a hoof for shoeing that the thought came to him. He finished the job, tied the horse at the hitching-rail outside the shop, and stood for a moment, looking up the street.

There were a few places in town from which almost everything could be seen. One of them was Greenwood's.

He hung up his apron, put on his coat and hat and started up the street.

# Chapter XIV

He paused in front of Holstrum's store, then walked over to where the would-be gunmen were shackled to the hitching-rail. He checked their shackles, then commented, "You boys should get wise to yourselves. If they ever brought off this job, how much would you get? The fewer there are around to split with, the bigger the shares for the others."

He pushed his derby back on his head. "Was I running this job I'd see you boys got turned loose just as the shooting starts. You'd help to create a diversion, and you'd get killed in the process."

Shanaghy knew too much about crooks not to know there was always mutual doubt and suspicion. "How well do you know the people you're working with?" he asked mildly. "I'd say you boys better be looking at your hole card."

"I don't know what he's talkin' about, do you, Turkey?" said one.

The thin, scrawny man shrugged. "Surely don't. We just come into town for a peaceful drink."

Shanaghy chuckled. "This here's a right deceiving town," he said. "For instance, I'd bet you boys don't know I've got men staked out all over town? And that when the shooting starts they'll be using shotguns and buffalo guns at close range?" He waved a hand around. "Boys, there ain't an inch of this street that isn't covered at less'n fifty yards, and mostly twenty yards, by shotguns and rifles. You boys are going to be right in the middle of a bloodbath."

Turkey shifted irritably. "What you gettin' at?"

"Only this . . . If you boys should be lucky enough to get loose or get turned loose before the shootin' starts,

I'd suggest you just leave out of here as fast as you can go."

"You make it sound like you got everything all figured out . . . whatever it is."

Shanaghy nodded. "That's just it. I have. And do you know why I'm tellin' you? Because you boys are just out to make a fast dollar. I don't figure you're so bad. And we don't want a lot of dead bodies when this is over . . . It's bad for business. What we'll do, of course, is scoop out a big ditch and just dump the lot of you in it, smooth her over and forget it."

Holstrum was coming down the street to open his store. Shanaghy nodded to him, "Mornin', Mr. Holstrum. Looks like a nice day. I was just fixin' to feed these boys."

Holstrum peered at them over his spectacles. "They look to be a rough lot," he said. "If you need any help—"

"They aren't that bad, Mr. Holstrum. Just some poor, misguided lads who won't be with us very long. I'll feed them well, Mr. Holstrum. They should at least have the pleasure of a last meal. It's a poor lot they are, but too young to pass on."

"You are going to *hang* them?" Holstrum asked.

"Oh, no!" Shanaghy looked terribly sad. "That won't be necessary. But when someone isn't needed any more . . . You know how that is, Mr. Holstrum? When people have outworn their usefulness . . . ?"

Holstrum peered at him over the glasses again. "Ah, Mr. Shanaghy! You have a good heart. Well, feed them well, then. If anything is said of the bill when it comes to the council, I will justify it."

"You, Turkey," Shanaghy said. "You first."

The stocky, dark-bearded one sat up. "You ain't feedin' us together?"

Shanaghy smiled. "That would be risky, wouldn't it? Ah, no, lads. One at a time. You know the old saying . . . 'two's company'? Just two of us alone, you know, it makes for better conversation."

"I ain't hungry," Turkey said.

"Too bad, because you're coming along anyway."

Shanaghy unshackled him, then put both cuffs on his wrists, "Come along, Turkey. You . . ." he looked back over his shoulder at the other, "just rest easy. Turkey an' me will have a nice talk. Then I'll come back for each of you."

When they were seated and had ordered, Shanaghy filled both their cups. "Feel sorry for you boys," he said. "After all, you're just trying for that fast dollar. You'd no way of knowing what you were gettin' into."

Turkey had a narrow face with snaky black eyes. He looked around, irritably. "Why don't you just shut up?"

Shanaghy smiled. "Ah, lad, don't be so short with a man who wishes you no ill. But that's the way of it. A man never knows who he can trust.

"It's a trap, you know," he said conversationally. "How do you suppose I know so much? I was tipped off," he said quietly, "by somebody who has got a scheme working within a scheme. This party has got it figured so they'll wind up with all the money. Actually," he commented, "it's a three-way cross. Some of those who think they are double-crossing you are actually being crossed themselves."

Shanaghy was just talking. He was trying to undermine Turkey's confidence, to weaken his resolution, to perhaps extract some clue. But as he talked he began to wonder if he hadn't stumbled upon the truth.

These men, probably like some others, were pawns in the game. But who were the principles? And how did they hope to bring it off?

Turkey ate sullenly. All of a sudden he slammed down his fork and swore. "Take me back, damn it!"

Shanaghy got to his feet. "Anybody can get himself into a hole," he commented. "But it takes a wise man to get out while the getting's good."

He took Turkey back and shackled him to the rail and led the stocky one to breakfast. When they were seated in the restaurant he let the man order, which he did, sullenly enough.

"What did Turkey tell you?" the man demanded, his eyes alight with suspicion.

"Turkey? Nothing at all. I didn't figure you boys knew much. After all, you're just here to create a disturbance and take a fall." Shanaghy smiled. "You boys stir up a dust while they ride out with the money."

"What money? I got no idea what you're talking about."

"Just eat," Shanaghy said. "I know all I need to know."

He asked no questions, made no overtures and obviously that worried the man even more than questions. Finally, Shanaghy did say, "You don't look much like a cowhand,"—although the man obviously did—"what did you do? Work on the railroad?"

"Hell," the man was disgusted, "what would you know about cowhands? I've ridden for some of the biggest outfits in Texas. Why, you just ask them and they'll tell you Cowan is—"

"All right, Cowan, you say you're a puncher, but I would think a cowhand would realize that people would see what horse he was riding and remember the brand. Yet you boys left your horses right in the street where anybody could see them."

"What d' you know about brands? Anyway, anybody can borry a horse."

"Of course." Shanaghy was remembering that he still had not discovered the missing horses. In the confusion of finding Carpenter's body and getting trapped in the burning barn, he had forgotten them. Yet where could they be? There were only two or three places left to look.

"How's he comin'? How's Sl—" he caught himself, then said, "You know? That gent you shot? The slim one?"

"Still alive. He's not conscious yet, however. I hope he stays unconscious until he's through talking."

Cowan glared at him from under thick brows. "Hell, you got somethin' on your mind about talkin'! You keep right on fishin', mister. You're going to come up with just nothing at all."

Cowan finished the coffee in his cup and wiped his mouth with the back of his hand. "How long you keepin' us out there?"

Shanaghy shrugged. "Until your boss turns you loose to get killed. Why go to the expense of trying you fellows when you will get yourselves killed by yourselves? When he turns you loose and the shooting's started, they'll take care of you."

"Who's 'they'?"

"Why, your friends, of course. The ones who roped you into this and now don't want to pay off. Everybody knows that when the shooting starts the action begins."

Shanaghy got up. "Come on . . . back you go. You've offered me nothing, so if you come out of this alive you'll be the one I hang it on." He grinned cheerfully. "Mr. Cowan, I'm going to need somebody, and if you survive I'll have you. Somebody will surely get killed and that will make it a hanging offense. Besides, the local boys haven't had a necktie party lately."

Shackling Cowan to the hitching-rail not far from Turkey, Shanaghy wandered back up the street. If he could get them to worrying enough, one of them might talk. At least when freed they might run. Yet he had accomplished nothing but to implant, he hoped, some element of doubt.

It was a warm, pleasant morning. A few scattered white tufts of cloud wandered across the blue of the sky. Shanaghy paused on the street and thought about New York.

Such a few days had passed since he'd been there, and yet the city was already vague and unreal in his thoughts. He wished suddenly he had the services of that old-timer who had taught him to shoot, wished he had him here to talk to. That was a shrewd old man. Or Morrissey or Lochlin . . . How was Lochlin?

And Childers? What had happened after he left? Childers, as he recalled, had some ties to the West, somewhere. They had supplied the muscle to put through some kind of land-fraud deal along the railroad.

He crossed the street when he saw Mrs. Carpenter. "Ma'am?" She paused. "I did some work at the shop, some stuff your husband had planned. If it's all right with you, ma'am, when this is over I'll either buy the shop from you or I'll buy half of it. And the horses, too," he added.

"He would have liked that, Mr. Shanaghy. He always said you were an excellent smith, that you'd missed your calling."

Shanaghy flushed. "Ma'am, I don't have no calling. I don't have a thing to speak of but a wish that keeps growing in me."

"A wish?"

"Yes, ma'am. A wish to be something more than I am, which isn't much. Maybe if I started with the shop—"

"When this is over, Mr. Shanaghy, we will talk." She paused. "Mr. Shanaghy, I always thought I was a Christian woman, but now all I want is to see the murderer of my husband caught and punished."

"So he shall be. Only don't speak of it now. Ma'am, there's somebody in town who's working with them, somebody . . . I don't know who."

He watched her walk away. Carpenter had been a good man, too good a man to die that way. Shanaghy started for the railroad station, then stopped. Josh Lundy was riding up the street.

"I reckoned you could use me. I got some work caught up so I come on in."

"You come alone?"

Josh looked down from his seat in the saddle. Wrinkles formed at the corners of his eyes. "Well, I set out mighty early . . . It's a fur piece from here to yonder."

"Did you come alone?" Shanaghy insisted.

"Pendleton was right busy, you might say. He did say he might come around later. His son was out on the range roundin' up some horses that done strayed off."

Tom Shanaghy waited, and when Josh said no more, he said, "Can you track?"

"A mite. I lived with the Pawnee one time. Picked up a little here an' yonder. What was it you wanted tracked?"

"A horse or two." Shanaghy explained about the three men who rode in, one of them on a Vince Patterson horse.

"Don't let that fret you. He left a couple of horses up here . . . at least, his brother did. I mean that time he got hisself killed. Somebody was holdin' those horses."

Shanaghy nodded. "All right, tie your horse and come along to the restaurant. I've got some things to talk over with you."

Josh nodded. "All right. You go right on in. I'll be along pretty soon. I'll take my horse down to the shop, an'—"

"Carpenter's dead. He was murdered."

"You don't say? Well, I ain't surprised. He was a good man, too good a man."

Shanaghy walked into the restaurant, removing his derby as he entered. He was halfway across the room when he saw her.

Jan Pendleton was sitting there facing him, and she was smiling. "Good morning. You look surprised."

"Josh didn't tell me—"

"He wouldn't." She looked up at him as he drew his chair back. "I rode in to see you."

"Me?" He was flustered. He drew back a chair and sat down.

"I heard you were having trouble," she said.

"Yes, ma'am. A mite. Here and yonder, as Josh would

say. First I was wishing you were here to be with Mrs. Carpenter after he was killed. You know, to have a woman about."

"I imagine her brother was with her. She wouldn't have needed me."

"Her brother?"

"Yes, didn't you know? He's the station agent. The telegrapher."

# Chapter XV

It was quiet in the little café. A few people came and went, but he scarcely noticed. Suddenly he was talking about his boyhood in Ireland, the things he remembered, the stories his father told him, about horses he had known . . . about the Maid o' Killarney.

"Are you returning to New York?" Jan asked.

He waited, thinking. "I don't know," he said at last. "Maybe I'll stay here. With Carp gone there's no smith. It is a good business but not exactly what I wanted."

"What do you want?"

There was that question again. He shifted uncomfortably. "I don't know, ma'am, I—"

"Call me Jan."

He looked up at her and for a moment their eyes met. He was embarrassed. "I'm Tom," he said.

"I know your name. I know more about you than you think."

"You don't. If you did you wouldn't even be talking to me."

Josh Lundy came in and crossed to their table. "Sorry to butt in, folks, but I have to talk to the marshal, here."

"Talk . . . And why didn't you tell me Jan rode in with you?"

Lundy widened his eyes. "Why, Marshal, I hadn't no idea you'd be interested. You figurin' to arrest her?"

"Sit down, Josh. If I could think of a charge, I'd shackle you to the rail along with the others, but I can't."

"Gimme a chance to catch up on my whittlin'," Josh replied. "I found them horses," he added, "at least, I found where they've been."

He pointed south. "There's a draw over yonder. Ain't much. Little corral over there and a lean-to. I done checked what tracks was left out behind where they first left their horses . . . I found two tracks like those in that old corral."

"Whose corral is it?"

"Nobody's. Built years back by some passerby with horses or cows to hold. She's only a hundred yards or so from here, but I reckon nobody in town goes there 'lest it's the youngsters. Some of them play Injun over there. One of those horses was a dark gray . . . unusual color. I found some hairs where he'd rubbed hisself on the snubbin' post."

Shanaghy thought about it. Yet he hesitated to ask the question. Finally, he did. "Josh, do you know whose horse that is? The dark gray one?"

"I do." He glanced at Jan, then dropped his eyes. "I guess ever'body does."

"It belongs to my brother," Jan said.

Shanaghy felt the sweat break out on his brow. He hesitated to speak, but Josh interrupted before he could frame any words.

"That doesn't say he rode it. Them horses been runnin' out. Anybody could rope up a horse an' it's often done, often of necessity. Folks don't really consider it stealin' unless somebody tries to ride out of the country or pens up a horse.

"Of course, a man who does that sort of thing better have a good explanation. I've roped up an' ridden other folks' horses many a time when mine played out, or I was in a gosh-awful hurry."

"There were a half dozen of Dick's horses running loose in a little pasture down by the creek," Jan said. "Father was saying the other day that they must be back in the brush, because he hadn't seen them the last few times he rode past."

"Was one of them a little black mare?"

"No." Jan smiled at him. "Was that what she was riding?"

"Holstrum has a black mare with two white stockings . . . pretty little thing."

"It sounds like the mare I saw."

Shanaghy was slowly putting things together. Suppose some strangers came into town and needed horses for a few days? Might they not catch up some they found running loose, use them and then turn them loose?

"Looks to me like I'd better do some riding around the country," he suggested.

"You tell me and I'll ride," Josh suggested. "Nobody would be surprised to see me. I'm always out roundin' up strays or whatever."

"All right . . . but watch yourself. Whoever is doing this doesn't intend to lose. They tried to trap me into a shoot-out where I'd be killed, and they've already killed Carpenter . . . I guess he got on to something."

"He was a friend of mine," Josh said quietly. "He was a man I liked."

"Josh," Shanaghy said, "maybe the best thing you could do right now would be just to talk about the people here. I don't know much about them. Just whatever you know about where they came from and what connections they have."

"We came from England," Jan said pertly. "We run a few cattle, and my father buys and sells cattle. My brother works with him."

"You know most of it," Josh said. "The town was started by Holstrum, Carpenter and Greenwood. They still own most of what's around here. Pendleton's got him a fine place. Holstrum and Greenwood both have a good bit of land around. They think highly of the town. Some folks don't.

"The three of them worked to get the railroad right-of-way where it is. Now they are working on the state capitol to get the town made the county seat. Judge McBane is with them on that, and so is Pendleton. If it goes through property values will go up."

"Tom," Jan was suddenly serious, "what are you going to do? I hear Uncle Vince is bringing his cattle up tomorrow."

"I've talked to him. He won't make trouble."

"Some of his hands might. When they get here, their job is finished. Some of them will go back to Texas to join another drive, but some will drift. Once they are paid off Uncle Vince no longer controls them."

"I'll have to handle that as it happens." Shanaghy looked up at her from the coffee cup. "I'm thinking about buying the blacksmith shop. Give me a toehold. A sort of place to start."

"Don't pay too much. Mrs. Carpenter is careful when it comes to money. When she sells anything she gets her money's worth. Papa told me that about her. She was angry when Carp first sold land here . . . said he should have leased it, instead."

"Holstrum wanted to buy her place," Lundy said.

"Her home, you mean?"

"She has a section of land south of here. It adjoins Holstrum's place and he wanted it, but she wouldn't sell. They had several long discussions about it but she wouldn't sell at all. I think Holstrum gave up.

"It was taken as grazing land but most of it is good farming land with a good spring and a small creek running through it."

"She proved up on it? What's that mean, exactly?" Shanaghy asked.

"Sink a well, plow some land, build a house, and then live on the land. They don't all do that. She'd go out there, time to time. Sometimes both of them would go but usually it was just her. Carp was busy with the shop."

"Did they build out there?"

Lundy shrugged. "Like they do . . . it was nothing much. Somebody had built a dugout, years ago. She fixed that up a mite and then had the fellow who takes care of Holstrum's place come over and build her a soddy . . . a sod house."

"I've never seen one."

"They just cut squares of sod and use them like bricks, then roof it over with poles. It makes a snug, warm place in winter when snow gets packed around it. But building one is more of an art than you'd figure. Takes some savvy."

"And Holstrum's man? He's good at it?"

"So they say. Name's Moorhouse. He's a good man with stock but damned unfriendly . . . Sullen sort, always packing a grouch. He's big and he's mean. Comes to town about once a month."

All the time Shanaghy sat there, he had the haunting feeling that he was missing something, that events were building in a way he did not suspect, that he was in deeper water than he could handle.

Josh made his excuses and left and they sat silent for awhile. Then Jan said, "I wish I could help."

"Just your being here helps," he admitted. He looked at her and shrugged. "I don't know what to do but wait and handle it as it comes."

"There isn't much else you can do." She paused. "Tom?

If Uncle Vince's men don't create a diversion of some kind, what will they do?"

"I think the robbers have planned for that. Maybe it will be an attempt to release those men I have shackled to the rail down there. Maybe it will be something else.

"When the train comes in and they unload the gold—"

"What if they don't unload it?"

That idea had passed through his mind before this. "You mean if they leave it on the train?"

"It's been planned so well, so what if they simply take the gold off elsewhere? If they have horses or a wagon waiting for them? What if there is a lot of shooting here in the streets and the train leaves?"

"But they'd have to get it off. Where would they unload?" Shanaghy asked.

"Let's get our horses. I'll show you where. It's only a little way."

They rode swiftly where the long winds blew, over the buffalo grass and the blue grama, here and there prairie flowers blooming. They startled a rabbit, then a small herd of antelope. To their right was the railroad, tracks shining bright in the sun.

They dipped into a hollow, then walked their horses up the far side. She rode well, this girl did, and she knew how to handle horses . . . But, like him, she had grown up with them.

She pulled up atop a small knoll.

"There!" she pointed. "I think that will be it."

A railroad construction shack, a pile of ties, a water tank. "They call it Holstrum. Before they had the water tank in town, they always stopped here for water, and they unloaded track materials there. Pa showed me," Jan added, "and Dick and I used to ride here and water our horses and rest before starting back.

"See?" She pointed. "There's a trail leading off across the country to the south, and another northwest."

"What lies off there?" Shanaghy pointed south.

"Holstrum's place. That's why they called it that. He owns most of this land aside from the right-of-way. He has a nice little cabin over there. Dick and I used to ride by sometimes, when we were younger. But since that mean Mr. Moorhouse has been there, we don't go anymore. Dick made me promise I wouldn't even ride this way."

"He's mean, you say. What's he like?"

"He's awfully big. Hulking. He has a mustache and he's always unshaved. He wears bib overalls, not the western kind, and he's dirty. He's very strong. I saw him pick up a whole barrel of vinegar once and put it on a wagon."

"A barrel of vinegar? Must weigh five hundred pounds!"

"I know. It took two very strong men to lift it off when we got it home. He was helping Mr. Holstrum in town then."

"Do you know Holstrum well?"

"Oh, I suppose so," Jan said. "He's a nice man, but lonely, I think. He still thinks of me as a little girl. I'd be uncomfortable around him if he didn't, I mean, from the way he looks at some girls.

"But ... I don't know. A few months ago there was a girl came to town ... Not a very nice one ... I think she worked in saloons and places like that. She tried to make up to him and he would have nothing to do with her."

Shanaghy chuckled. "He's got his sights set higher. He wants a lady, a real lady. He told me once about one ... the kind he liked ... smelling of nice perfume, and very ladylike and ..."

He stopped abruptly and they looked at each other. "Tom? Do you think—? Could it be? That girl. The one you saw in the restaurant? She looks like a lady, and she does use very good scent. I mean—"

"Jan ... don't look now, and don't stop. Just keep riding but bear off a little to the north."

"What's wrong?"

"There's somebody there ... at the water tower. He's watching us!"

# Chapter XVI

The water tower was no more than two hundred yards off and the man had a glass. Shanaghy could see the reflected light from it. He was watching them. Fortunately they had not been riding straight toward the tank but a little north of it, planning to turn when they reached the trail.

"Keep right ahead until we reach the trail, then turn north."

"But who could it be?" Jan asked.

"I'd like to know, but I suspect this would not be a good time to go nosing around."

"You'd ride right down there if I weren't here," she protested.

"Maybe . . . But I want them all, not just one man. I want the man who killed Carpenter."

"If it was a man."

"What?" He glanced at her. "What do you mean by that?"

"Women can commit crimes, too. Carpenter was in somebody's way, and I don't think it was only because he was about to find the horses. I think he was in the way anyhow."

Shanaghy glanced out of the corners of his eyes toward the water tower. The man was no longer using the glass but had picked up a rifle.

They rode down a slight bank into the trail and turned north, away from the water tank. Desperately, Shanaghy wished to look back, but he forced himself not to turn his head even the slightest. The trail was one rarely used and showed no recent evidence of travel, so those at the water tank must have come in along the tracks or from the south.

"A little faster," he said. How far were they now? Three hundred yards? No, not quite so much.

They topped a rise and dropped over into a small hollow through which ran a stream. There, at the edge of a clump of willows, a man sat on a boulder.

He was bearded and old, wearing a moth-eaten coonskin cap, fringed buckskin pants and a checked black and white shirt. In his hands he carried a rifle, and over his back a pack in which there was a blanket and poncho.

"Howdy, folks! Nice day!" He noted the badge. "Ha? Marshal, is it? Well, it's about time some of you fellers picked up their sign."

They drew up. "Whose sign?"

"You mean you ain't seen 'em? I mean that triflin' lot who're down yonder by the tank. Lucky this here stream's here or a body couldn't even fetch hisself a drink."

"What d'you know about them?"

"Know? I know all I need to know. They're rough folks. Kill you soon as look at you. They done shot at me."

"When?"

"Three, four days back. Some city feller down yonder by the water tank, he said I was to git away an' not come back.

"I ast if'n he was the railroad, and he said he wasn't but he spoke for them. I ast him if he spoke for Big Mac and he said that made no difference, I was to git. I told him Big Mac said I could have all the water I needed, and he said he was tellin' me I couldn't.

"Well, I could see he didn't know Big Mac, and he surely had nothin' to do with the road, an' I told him so. He ups with a six-shooter and told me to hightail it, and I done so.

"Right then I knowed somethin' was almighty wrong, because Big Mac is division superintendent of this line an' ever'body knows him. Nobody who works for that road would speak slighting of Big Mac . . . He'd skin 'em alive. An' Mac is a friend of mine. Me an' his pa prospected together.

"So I kept nosin' around an' they seen me. I surely wasn't hidin' . . . No reason to . . . An' one of them waved me off, then this city feller . . . My eyes is still good for distance . . . He ups with his rifle and killed my burro. He killed ol' Buster . . . Buster, he been with me nine, ten year. Killed him . . . creased me.

"Well, Marshal, I ain't about to leave. Not until I get me one of them. Hopeful, it'll be that city feller. I had him true in my sights the other day, an' then that woman come between us. She—"

"What woman?"

"Her who brings 'em grub sometimes. I seen her come over there a time or two, sometimes with a rig an' sometimes a'horseback."

"Young, pretty woman?"

"Sort of. Depends on what a man calls purty an' what he calls young. But attractive, I'd say, mighty attractive."

The old man peered at Shanaghy. "You're that there new feller I've heard talk of. Come right in and come to be marshal right off."

"Nobody else wanted the job."

"I reckon not. Not with Rig hurtin' like he is."

Shanaghy had been about to ride on, but the words pulled him up short. "Rig hurting, you say?" He studied the old man. "You talk like you know where he is."

"I should smile, I do! Nobody knows no better!" The old man chuckled. "Him a'frettin' an' a'sweatin' over all this here, an' me tellin' him not to worry, that you got it under *con*-trol!"

"Where is he?"

The old man cocked his head. "Where? Now wouldn't you like to know? I reckon them fellers down to the tank would give a purty penny to know just where he's at."

He chuckled again, looking very wise. "They *had* him. Had him dead to rights. All lashed up like one o' them Christmas packages, an' I snuck in an' fetched him away!"

He chuckled again. "You should have seen 'em! Like chickens with their heads off, runnin' all over, here an' yonder! An' that woman, she was fit to be tied! Read 'em the riot act, she did!"

Tom Shanaghy held very still. He glanced over at Jan. Her eyes were wide and she was caressing her horse's neck, fooling with the mane. "I'd like to see him," she said. "Is he all right? I mean, wasn't he hurt?"

"*Hurt?* You're darn tootin', he was hurt! They figured they had him killed, but they didn't want him *found*. They figured to have him disappear, like. I reckon so's they'd figure him still around. That way the folks in town wouldn't latch onto somebody to take his place. Like they done you."

He chuckled. "That must've upset 'em! Upset 'em plenty! You comin' in out of nowhere, actin' like you was sent!"

He peered at Shanaghy. "Can't figure out why they ain't kilt you."

"They've tried."

"I should reckon." The old man bobbed his head. "You get through this night . . . you're shot with luck. Up to now they been foolin'. Now they got to git shut of you."

He looked around at Jan. "You're wishful to see Rig Barrett? I'll take you to him."

"Thanks," Shanaghy said, "I was going to ask—"

"Hey, there! Pull up, now! Nobody said nothin' about takin' *you* to him. It was *her*. She done asked an' she's worried about him. I'll take her. Not you."

"But—"

"It's all right, Tom," Jan said. "I'll be all right."

"All right? I should reckon!" The old man peered at Shanaghy. "Jealous, are you? Jealous of old Coonskin, are you? Well, I don't blame you! Here a few year back I used to cut quite a figure amongst the gals! Nobody could dance the fandango like ol' Coonskin Adams! Them gals . . . why, they was all just a'pantin' around after me!

"Looks I ain't got, but I do got *style!* Yes, siree-bob! I got style!"

He turned on Jan. "You come along with me, young lady. I'll take you to Rig. This here marshal, he can do whatever he's of a mind to, but he should watch hisself because tonight's the night! They'll kill him tonight. They don't want nothin' to mess with their big day. An' Rig, he's in no shape to fetch 'em."

"Coonskin," Shanaghy said seriously. "I need to talk to Rig. I need his advice. Look, I don't know what I'm walkin' into."

"You're a'doin' fine. Just you don't trust nobody. *Nobody*, d'you hear?"

They rode away, and Shanaghy watched them go, torn with doubt. That young, beautiful girl, going off with a rough, dirty-looking old man . . . to where?

Turning his horse, he started back to town. As he rode he slowly reviewed what he knew and what he suspected.

The projected robbery had begun either in the mind of someone in town who knew about the money that would be arriving, or someone who had access to the information from other sources. Shanaghy knew enough about crime and criminals to know that no information is really secret. There is always somebody who knows, and there is always somebody who will talk—in the strictest confidence, of course, but talk they will. And if one talks, another will.

A quarter of a million dollars is a lot of money. Vince Patterson's herd would bring him perhaps sixty thousand dollars, but there were other herds not far behind. The money would be needed to cash checks, to pay off hands, and to keep the wheels of trade turning at their proper speed. A large portion of that money would be spent right in town . . . if it wasn't stolen.

How many men were involved? There was at least one man at the water tower, but there had been all those others, too. George, the man on the train, the three men shackled to the hitching-rail . . . and a woman.

There had to be somebody in town. No outsider had smuggled those horses away so quickly.

Turning his horse he cut across the prairie away from the railroad, riding northwest. The prairie was not as flat as it seemed from town, being gently rolling in places with a good many dips and hollows. Here and there was a stream-bed, most of them dry. Standing in his stirrups and looking back, he could see nothing of Jan or the old man. They had vanished as if they had never been.

He rode into town from the north. As he entered he saw Mrs. Carpenter shading her eyes at him from her door, but when he made as if to ride toward her she went inside and closed the door.

A man whom he recognized as one who worked for the lumberyard was standing in the street as if waiting. Shanaghy pulled up. "Something wrong?" he asked.

"Miz Carpenter wants her horse. That there one you're ridin'."

"Carpenter loaned it to me. He said—"

"Maybe he said. Anyway, Carpenter is dead, as you mighty well know. That there horse belongs to Miz Carpenter, an' she wants it back."

There was no friendliness in the man. "She wants it back, an' she wants it now."

"I'll leave it at the stable."

"Mister, I said she wants it *now*. Right here . . . *now*."

Surprised and irritated, Shanaghy dismounted. "Why, sure. Although I don't see what she's in such a hurry for."

"You don't? Mister, there's folks around askin' themselves questions about how Carpenter comes to be dead, and you with the body, and all.

"You come in here out of nowhere and start workin' with him. You see he's got him a nice business there. You start ridin' around on his horse, in a saddle belonging to him, and you even work there when he's not around, collectin' money for work and materials and all. Then suddenly Carp, who didn't have an enemy in the world, is found dead."

The eyes were cold and accusing. "Found dead by you . . . And you say you escaped from a burning barn that somebody set afire.

"Now does that make sense? Who would lock you in a barn and set it afire? Who would kill Carp? Who stood to gain by it?"

"You're mistaken, my friend," said Shanaghy. "I liked Carp, and he liked me, we—"

"You say. But who stood to gain? You're the only smith around. Hear you been cozening up to Miz Carpenter, too.

"Mister, you may think you're some shakes, walkin' around with that badge and all. Well, let me tell you . . ."

Shanaghy fought down an angry reply. "Take the horse and saddle to Mrs. Carpenter and thank her for me. I guess I'll just have to find another horse."

"Not in this town, you won't."

Angrily, Shanaghy strode up the street to the hotel. What in God's name was happening? Had she gone crazy?

A man standing in front of Holstrum's turned abruptly away as he approached, and another deliberately walked across the street, away from him.

Shanaghy pushed open the door and entered the hotel, starting for the stairs. Suddenly he stopped. His gear . . . or, rather, Rig's gear and his few extra clothes, were bundled up at the bottom of the stairs.

He looked up to find the clerk smiling at him, a malicious smile. That clerk had never liked him, anyway.

"Sorry, Mr. Marshal-man. We needed your room. You'll have to look somewhere else."

The clerk leaned his elbows on the desk. "We don't want your kind around here, mister. My advice to you is get while the getting is good. They can't prove anything right now, but they will. And when they do, you'll hang. You'll *hang!* D'you hear me?"

# Chapter XVII

Shanaghy emerged upon the street, shaken by the sudden twist events had taken. He stood for a minute or two, his gear beside him, trying to adjust to the situation.

He had been warned they would try to kill him, and they still might. But what they were doing now was many times more effective, or so it seemed to him. The townspeople he was trying to aid and protect had turned against him.

They believed him a murderer, and he had to admit that looking at things the way they were, such a theory was plausible.

Now he had no horse, no place to sleep, and he doubted if he could even buy a meal. Who had started the story? By the time he figured that out, it would be already too late. Whatever was going to happen here would happen within the next few hours.

Taking up his gear he went down the street to Holstrum's store. The store was empty when he entered except for Holstrum himself, who peered at him from over his glasses.

"I need a place to stay," Shanaghy said. "They put me out at the hotel."

The storekeeper shrugged. "I have nothing for you." His manner was cool. "My advice is to leave . . . while it is still possible. You are not liked here. Since you have come much has happened, and there are many who believe you yourself killed poor Mr. Carpenter. My advice is to go . . . before enough men get together to hang you."

A moment Shanaghy hesitated, but Holstrum had turned away. Taking up his gear he walked out to the street again.

It was impossible, and yet . . . it had happened. Who had started the rumor? And why?

Maybe it was only an idea that started in the mind of an overwrought and grief-stricken woman. And maybe it was an idea put there by somebody who saw a chance to destroy him . . . or at least to get him out of town.

Shanaghy thought suddenly of his prisoners. He must have walked right by them, unthinking. He looked again.

They were gone.

Greenwood . . . He would go to Greenwood.

One man was finishing a beer as he entered. The man glanced at him, put a coin on the bar and walked out.

Shanaghy stepped up to the bar. "How about it? Are you shutting me out, too?"

Greenwood's features were expressionless. "What'll you have?"

"Beer."

Greenwood drew the beer and placed it before him. "It's a small community, and stories get around. Carpenter's been murdered. Folks start asking who stood to gain by it, and your name came up first. Carp was a well-liked man. He'd had no trouble before. You come to town, you work at his shop and suddenly he's dead . . . You find his body, but the barn where he was killed burned, and with it all the evidence."

Greenwood glanced at Shanaghy. "You had anything to eat?"

"No . . . and I'm hungry."

"Don't have much here, but I can give you a bowl of chili and some crackers." He dished it up. "Lived in Tucson a good many years back. All you could get in a restaurant there in those days was chili, chili and beans or beef. You'd think I'd be sick of it, but I'm not."

Greenwood put the bowl of steaming chili and another bowl filled with oyster crackers on the bar. "You want to know what I think? I don't believe you murdered Carp. I do know he liked you, and I think you did him . . . well as you knew him."

"We talked a little. I did like him."

Greenwood lit a cigar. "You've got enemies, and if I feed you they'll be my enemies."

"I'll stay away."

"You needn't." Greenwood puffed thoughtfully at the

cigar. "In this case your enemies have to be my enemies.
I mean those who aren't just misguided but real enemies."

Greenwood took Shanaghy's beer from the bar and put
a head on it. "That's partly my money coming in on the
train."

"How much of it is yours?"

"The big part. I've got a hundred and fifty thousand
coming in. Other businessmen around town have maybe
another fifty. Carp has some and so does Holstrum."

"I don't comprehend. Why is so much of it yours?"

"We wanted the cattle business and I had access to
more cash than the others. Good credit. So I agreed to
carry the weight of it."

Shanaghy looked at Greenwood thoughtfully, then went
on with his eating. He was hungry and the chili tasted
good . . . very good. Yet there was a feeling that he was
missing something, and a feeling of impending doom.

"Greenwood," Shanaghy said suddenly, "if I were you
I'd close up shop and keep out of sight. I think your
number is up, too."

"Mine?"

"You just said most of that money was yours. By coming into the picture I've messed up their plans. I don't
think they intended to kill anyone . . . Maybe they didn't
. . . except for Rig. Then when I came into the picture they had to kill me. Well, they haven't done it so
far but they'll keep trying.

"Now, they're trying to run me out of town. They've
taken my room from me. I've no place to eat, and they've
taken my horse. I'd lay a bet I can't even get a ticket
out of town, although maybe they'd be glad to see me
go."

"What's happening, then?"

"It's somebody right here in town who is mixed up in all
this. I tell you, man, they had it all worked out, until
Rig Barrett smelled something rotten." Shanaghy paused,
then asked, "Whose idea was it to hire Rig?"

"Mine. Judge McBane agreed. So did Carpenter. Holstrum did, then he worried about it, afraid we'd get a
worse lawman than we had. He voted against it finally."

"Carp was for it?"

"He was."

Shanaghy finished the chili and drank the last of the beer.

"You'd better hole up. I can't promise you where I'll be, but they shan't drive me out. I'll find a horse somewhere—"

"I have several. Take your pick. And there's all the gear you'll need, right out back." Greenwood reached under the bar and pulled out a shotgun. "I have this, and if you need me—"

"You just stay here. I may need a place to come to."

He paused, looking up the empty street. It was too empty . . . and that worried him. "Greenwood, how well do you know Mrs. Carpenter?"

The saloon-keeper looked up the sunlit street where the dust stirred briefly. "Not much." He spoke reluctantly, as one who did not talk about women, at least about decent women. "She kept pretty much to herself . . . Didn't socialize a lot. Folks seemed to like her, but . . . well, she was stand-offish.

"Carp was different. He liked folks, enjoyed sitting around talking. He was a serious man, though, and knew what he was about. Sometimes . . ." he hesitated, "sometimes I figure she thought she was a mite too good for all of us, Carp included."

"And her brother?"

"They were close. Saw a lot of one another, but he wasn't a mixer, either. He'd come in here, time to time, and buy a bottle." He scowled. "Come to think of it, here lately he's been buying more. Sometimes two or three bottles at a time."

"Becoming a drunk?"

"I never saw him drunk. No . . . I don't think so."

"How about other stuff? Groceries?

Greenwood shrugged. "No . . . Holstrum would be the only one would know about that."

"I was wondering . . . Maybe he was buying that whiskey for somebody else? Somebody who didn't want to show up around town?"

Shanaghy got up. Greenwood rinsed out the bowls and his beer mug, then dried his hands on his apron. It was cool and pleasant in the small saloon. Shanaghy looked up the street. Already the buildings looked weather-beaten and old. Sun, wind and blown sand would do that. In the prairie country, towns had a way of aging very fast.

The wind picked up a little dust and carried it along, then dropped it. A horse tied at the hitching-rail stamped his feet and blew through his nostrils. Shanaghy missed the clang of the hammer from the smithy.

Carp had been a good man, a solid man. And now he was dead . . . just when he had been trying to help, too.

Was that the reason? Was it just that he was in the way?

Tom Shanaghy stirred restlessly, irritably. He was out of his depth. What *was* going on here, anyway? His thoughts strayed to New York and Morrissey. At least he knew there who his enemies were. Yet now it all seemed so far, far away.

He had wanted no trouble when he came here. He wanted only to board the train and leave. He had even bought his ticket . . . and he could still do that, he could do it tomorrow—if somebody would sell him one . . .

Suddenly his eye caught a flicker of movement up the street. There was a man standing in the deepest shade of the awning in front of the express office. The man had a rifle.

Shanaghy watched for a minute or two, his eyes slowly sweeping the scene before him, his mind racing. They were ready for him. They were all set to kill him, and now they had undoubtedly enlisted some of the good men of the town as well, convincing them that he had killed Carpenter.

Walking into a cold deck like that was not to his liking. He glanced around at Greenwood. "Close up and hole up, and don't let anybody in unless it's me." He paused a minute. "Greenwood, I'm beginning to get the pattern. You were to be the patsy all along. I mean, maybe they started out with other ideas but it was your money they wanted. I'm going to take one of your horses and slip out of town. I'm going to ride to Patterson's outfit for help."

Greenwood shifted the shotgun from one hand to the other, nodding slowly. "All right, Shanaghy, I'll stand pat. But for God's sake get back here."

Greenwood put the shotgun on the bar and mopped his brow. "They won't let you get out of town, Shanaghy. By now they are watching my horses. They might think you'd run but they dasn't take the chance."

Tom Shanaghy was of the same notion. He stared up

the street, trying to fit all the pieces together. There had to be somebody in town . . . Who?

The idea that kept nagging at him made no sense, yet it could fit . . . it did fit. In part at least. If he just knew who his enemies were, he would know better how to proceed.

"What about Holstrum?" he asked suddenly.

Greenwood shrugged. "He stands to lose, too. Anyway, I can't see him figuring this out."

"Some of those big, slow men are damn smart," Shanaghy said. "It doesn't pay to underrate them." He was looking up the street and thinking. They didn't have much time.

He swore bitterly. "Hell of it is, there's some good but mistaken men out there. I don't want to kill anybody who doesn't have it coming."

He looked around. "Greenwood, that girl's in it, I know, and so's that George whatever-his-name-is. But who was it turned the town against me? It surely wasn't one of them. It had to be a local. It had to be somebody folks would listen to."

"Who, then?"

Shanaghy turned his head and stared at him. "They would listen to you, Greenie."

Greenwood shrugged. "It wasn't me. Like you've said, most of that money will be mine. I stand to lose it all. I stretched my credit, Shanaghy. I'll be broke if we lose that money . . . wiped out."

"The judge?"

"Him? Not on your life! He's a solid man, an honest man. If there was one man in town . . ."

Greenwood paused. "Shanaghy, that young woman you spoke of? The one who met the gambler? You said she seemed to come from the south?"

"Aye . . . and that was a thing I wished to speak to him about . . . Carpenter knew her horse, I am sure of it."

Greenwood poured them each a beer. He rested his hands on the bar and wet his lips with his tongue. Then reluctantly he said, "Holstrum has a place down that-away."

"I know. I've been thinking of that. And Holstrum voted against Rig Barrett being brought in."

Shanaghy watched up the empty street. There were two riflemen in sight now, watching the saloon. He had a hunch the back was no better. He glanced at the clock. Almost an hour . . . but what could he do? To venture out was to get shot. They were going to win. They were going to defeat him, after all. How had he ever been such a fool as to believe he could bring this off? What experience did he have that qualified him to step into Rig Barrett's shoes? But who else had there been?

He thought of Jan. She had ridden off with that strange old man, supposedly to see Rig . . . Where? Did her father and brother know where she was? Her brother? What kind of a bungling fool was he, anyway?

Where was Josh Lundy? And where did he stand now? Restlessly, he paced the floor, watching every window, every door. Nobody was on the street. As if on signal all shopping seemed to have ceased. No rigs were tied along the street.

Nothing could be better for the thieves. Now they had it all their own way, better even than planned. There would be no fight between the town and Vince Patterson, but Shanaghy, the only officer, was pinned down in the saloon and without allies. Fearful of shooting that might develop, the townsfolk had deserted the streets. So the train would come in with its shipment, it would be unloaded at the platform and the train would depart. The gold would be in the hands of the thieves without a chance of interference.

Greenwood, who was to receive the shipment, was also pinned down. Instead of a few fast minutes of work, now they could take their time. The thought irritated Shanaghy. They were so sure now that he was whipped.

Was he?

He swore again, suddenly, bitterly, and Shanaghy was not a man who was inclined to swear. He looked down the empty street. The train would be coming, the gold would be taken from it, the train would go on. Yet what would they do with the gold? Where would it be taken?

"I think Holstrum is in it," he said, suddenly. "I think he has been a part of it from the first. It may even have been his idea."

Greenwood said nothing. He looked into his beer, then swallowed some of it.

"It's the woman," Shanaghy said. "It is because of her. Or maybe Holstrum is tired of this," he said, waving a hand around. "He may want to leave."

"He was unhappy here at first," Greenwood admitted. "He got into it, but things did not move swiftly enough. I believe he expected the town to grow faster, the values to increase. And then," he shrugged, "there was something the town did not give him, something he wanted."

Shanaghy glanced again at the clock. Only a few minutes had passed. He walked back to the bar and finished his own beer.

What would Morrissey have done? Shanaghy didn't know but he had an idea Morrissey would have walked out there and dominated the situation by sheer personality. So would Rig Barrett.

He looked into his empty glass, thinking. Suddenly, his thoughts turned to the water tower. Why were those men so anxious to keep people away? What did the water tower have to do with their plans?

Suppose they had never intended to bring the gold into town? Suppose it was to have been unloaded there, at the water tower, and spirited away from there while confusion existed in town? Jan had suggested it.

If Holstrum was involved, that would make sense. His place was not far off and he had horses, and probably a buckboard or wagon.

"I don't like any of this." He turned on Greenwood. "There's something going on here . . . I don't know what it is. There are too many of the wrong people involved, and I can't believe they are the kind to share. They all seem greedy to me."

He shook his head irritably. "Oh, I know it is all imagination! I don't *know* anything! But I do know what I feel and I've mixed with that kind for half my life! They have a plan . . . But it doesn't feel right to me, so I am thinking somebody else has a separate plan."

"Tom?" Greenwood pointed. "Look!"

Shanaghy turned sharply. A young man in a white buckskin vest was dismounting up the street.

Win Drako!

Bass was with him, tying his horse close by. Bass looked over his shoulder toward the saloon and said something to Win Drako.

A door opened up the street and Drako himself appeared. "It will be a day to remember," Tom Shanaghy said softly, "if a man lives past it!"

"They're coming for you," Greenwood said.

"Who else?"

"There's three of them."

"Aye! 'Tis a thing to think on, Greenwood. Three!"

"They're coyotes," Greenwood said contemptuously. "They kept from sight until they knew the whole town was against you, and then they come!"

"Ah, but the advantage is mine," Shanaghy said. "They are fools."

"The advantage is yours? Are you crazy?"

"No, Greenie," Shanaghy said. "A man who stands alone is the stronger because he knows he has no one on whom to lean. He must do it all himself. When there are more than one, each is expecting the other to get it done. Each holds back a little, hoping not to get hurt."

He smiled. "It is a favor they have done me, Greenie, a favor indeed. For it is my means to get out of here in one piece. Those others, you see, they will stand back to watch. They will watch to see the Drakos kill me."

"Do you want the shotgun?"

"Keep it. You may need it, man, and I shall do what must be done with a six-shooter. However, I could use another if you have it."

"You're really going out there?"

"Aye." He took the gun Greenwood handed him, glanced to see if it was loaded. "Aye, I am going out, and I shall keep going, me lad! I shall go until this is done with and then I'll be going back to New York."

He paused a moment, his hand on the latch. The three men up the street stood together, talking, glancing from time to time at the saloon.

"They will be expecting me there, for I wrote a note to Morrissey. I wished him to know that I had not run out on him, and I told him I'd be back when this was over. Have a care for yourself, Greenie." He lifted the latch.

Up the street the three men had spread out and were walking toward the saloon.

# Chapter XVIII

He should feel fear, but he did not. He should be wary, but he was not. The three men walking toward him were coming to kill. Their one intent was to kill him, to shoot him down.

He was disturbed that he was not afraid, for all good sense told him he should be. Three to one . . . the odds were long.

Suddenly he remembered something. There were two other Drakos . . . Dandy and Wilson. He had not seen them but he had heard of them. The moment he thought of them he knew he was in trouble—far deeper trouble than came from just the three men headed toward him.

They were the window dressing, they were the ones to draw his attention. The others would be nearby . . . ambushed, waiting.

Five . . . It was too many. Sweat beaded his forehead but still, he told himself, he was not afraid. He felt a strange sort of triumph. This was something with which he could deal. He was not by nature a plotter or planner. He liked straightforward enemies with whom he could deal in a straightforward way.

Holstrum's store . . . One or more of them would be there, waiting. From the tail of his eye he caught the slightest of movements. He had taken only three steps out from the store, ahead and to the side. Now the awning posts were on his left, slim trunks of cottonwood holding up the awning. He was a little in the shadow, the three men before him in the bright sun. Then he saw the other man, standing on the steps of the hotel. He had a rifle in his hands and he was lifting it.

The man in Holstrum's store suddenly stepped out. Shanaghy caught a fleeting glimpse of the man, wearing a black vest and a red handkerchief about his neck, and then he went for his gun.

As he did so he heard a sharp cry from his right and up the street. *"Win!"* It was Josh Lundy's voice.

And then Shanaghy was firing. He shot over Drako's head at the man on the hotel steps with the rifle. And without glancing to see what effect his shot had, he turned right and shot at the man on the store steps.

His action was swift and totally unexpected, in that both men believed all his attention was on the men before him. At the same moment he heard a burst of gunfire from right and left, and he saw Win Drako down in the dust and Bass running, hands in the air.

Drako was looking at him, lifting his gun. But there was something wrong with Drako, the gun was coming up too slowly. Another shot from the left and Drako turned half around and fell.

In the distance, a train whistled.

Shanaghy saw Josh Lundy come into the street, rifle in hand, and Josh was walking toward the two men down in the street, walking cautiously.

From the other side came a tall young man in a black hat and coat, a man he did not know.

He walked toward Shanaghy, shifting his rifle to his left hand. He held out the right. "Am I always to be getting you out of trouble?" he asked.

Shanaghy stared. There was something familiar, yet . . .

"On the pier, in New York," the man said. "We were boys then and John Morrissey saved our bacon."

"Well, I'll be damned! I—!"

"I am Dick Pendleton . . . Jan's brother. It's been a long time."

The train whistled again, nearer.

Shanaghy grabbed Pendleton's hand, then suddenly everything started to fall into place.

"Dick! Another time!" He ran for Drako's horse, jerked loose the slip knot and sprang to the saddle.

The water tank! Of course, they'd be doing it there and never coming into the station at all. It was only after he cleared the town that he began to realize what he was letting himself in for.

There would be several of them. The women . . . women? Why had he thought that? Then he knew—because

there had to be two women. He couldn't make it out
otherwise.

Two women who might or might not be present. There'd
be George, and George, he thought, would be good with
a gun. Used to using one, at least. There'd be the man
who had posed as the brakeman . . . and how Shanaghy
wanted to see *him*. He'd made him jump off a freight into
darkness. Shanaghy had never wanted to kill a man, and
he didn't want to kill that brakeman, but he would like
to give him a taste of what he'd had.

He slowed his pace. He would be within sight of the
train in a minute.

He had forgotten to ask Dick Pendleton about Jan. Was
she home? Was she safe? The thought that he had forgotten left him feeling guilty. And that old man . . .
Coonskin . . . who wanted a shot at the eastern dude.
Where was he?

When he topped the hill he saw the train. It was
pulled up at the water tank and was taking on water.
There was nobody around.

Had he guessed wrong? Would he have to turn and race
back into town again?

He rode down the hill and pulled up, looking at the
train. It was longer than usual, at least eight cars. An
express car, a baggage car, a passenger car and five freight
cars, as well as a caboose.

He checked his guns and flushed with embarrassment. He
had forgotten to reload.

He did so now. There was a rifle in the saddle-scabbard,
too. What had Win been shooting with? He could not
recall. It had happened so fast, there'd been no time to
consider anything, even to notice.

Those two men he'd shot. Both had gone down and
they must have been the other sons of Drako.

There was some activity on the other side of the train.
He heard somebody swear and heard the rattle of trace-
chains. His heart was pounding. When that train started to
move . . .

How many would there be? Too many.

Suddenly a brakeman appeared and gave a signal. The
train whistled, then started taking up slack. Then slowly
it chugged forward. On the far side of the train the wagon
was also moving.

He drew his gun.

The rifle was probably loaded and ready but he felt more at ease with a six-gun. The train started forward and he walked his horse. He was ready, poised. Suddenly the train started to back up. It backed a dozen yards, then stopped, the locomotive puffing contentedly.

Swearing, he rode toward the rear, planning to ride behind the train. It started backing up again. He wheeled his horse, rode alongside the train and leaped for the ladder. He scrambled up the ladder as the train suddenly jerked to a stop, before spinning its wheels and starting forward again. He ran forward along the car tops. Suddenly a bullet clipped near his feet. It had been fired from the engine. Shanaghy fired back and heard the clang of the bullet as it struck, somewhere in the cab.

Another bullet whipped by him and he dropped to the top of the car, clinging tightly with his one free hand. He fired again and then leaped up, ran forward and sprang down to the tender atop the coal pile.

The engineer held a gun in his hand, one hand on the throttle.

"Drop it!" Shanaghy said. An instant the engineer hesitated, then let go of the pistol.

Shanaghy scooped it up, then said, "Now back up, carefully . . . slowly."

"What is this? A holdup?"

"You know damn well what it is," Shanaghy said.

He glanced toward the road that led south. The road was empty as far as he could see. Win Drako's horse was grazing beside the road.

"You," he said to the engineer. "When you get to town, you go to Greenwood's and report to him and tell him what has happened and what you've done."

The engineer stared at him unbelieving. "You think I'll do that?"

"I do." Shanaghy smiled at him, and it was not a pleasant smile. "You do it. If you don't, or if you try to get away, I'll come after you."

The engineer shrugged. "You ain't done so well so far. Maybe I ain't scared."

"You ask them in town how well I have done. But look, mister, I'm not persuading you. I really don't give a damn what you do, but if I have to come after you you'll wish you'd shot yourself first."

He swung down and walked toward the horse. It looked

up at him and started to walk off. Shanaghy spoke gently. The horse stopped, looking at him again, and he caught up the reins and stepped into the saddle.

The tracks of a wagon were in the road, if one could call it that. For it was merely two wheel tracks leading off to the south. Such a wagon could not be far ahead, but he still had no idea how many men were with it. Yet when he crossed the next rise there was no sign of the wagon at all.

The wagon and its cargo had vanished!

Ahead of him lay open road, visible for over a mile, with only a few dips. And there was nothing in sight. The road itself and the plains around it were empty. He rode on, more swiftly, dipping into a dry wash where the banks were caving badly, then up the opposite side.

Nothing . . .

The gently rolling plains stretched far away, and there was nothing in sight but a few cattle, feeding on the drying grass.

He slowed down. Something was wrong, radically wrong.

There had been a wagon. He had seen its tracks. He *knew* he had.

But now there were no tracks!

For a moment he sat very still, simply staring. It was no illusion. There simply were no wagon tracks in the road. Not fresh ones, at least.

He rode right and left on the prairie but found nothing. He swung wide in a big circle . . . Still nothing.

Irritably, he rode on, searching for some sign of a wagon passing, but he found nothing. So, he thought, the wagon had turned off. Swinging his horse around, he rode back.

He found the tracks again, then lost them in the wash with the caving banks. A moment of digging and he found the wagon, wheels pulled off, the wagon-bed lying flat . . . and empty.

There were horse tracks some fifty yards from where he found the wagon, a place where several horses had been tied. He found tracks, but nothing else distinguishable.

He was no tracker and he made no attempt at it now. He rode straight for the cabin that Holstrum had on his claim, where the man named Moorhouse was the caretaker.

There was a small cabin, a stable, and a corral. In the corral were several horses, none of them showing signs of having been recently ridden. As he pulled up in the yard the cabin door opened and a big man came out. And he was very big.

He came out of the door slipping a suspender over his shoulder. "You lookin' for somethin'?"

Shanaghy touched the badge on his chest. "I have to search the place."

The big man came into the middle of the yard. "You'll play hell. If you know what's good for you, you'll git!"

"Sorry, I have to search the place, Mr. Moorhouse."

"Know my name, huh?"

"Of course. The law knows such things."

"Then you should damn well know that tin badge ain't worth nothin' outside of town. And not very much in it."

Shanaghy smiled. "I'd hate to have to put you in jail for obstructing the law."

Moorhouse laughed harshly. "You arrest *me?*"

"That's right." Shanaghy was smiling. "But I'll have a look at the stable first."

"Mister," Moorhouse said, "I given you a chance. You git out of here *now* or they won't be enough left of you to pick up with a sponge."

Shanaghy smiled. "You know, Mr. Moorhouse, I like you. Now I'm going to search the premises, and if you obstruct me I'm going to throw you in jail. We haven't any courthouse and we haven't any city hall and we haven't any jail, but I can shackle you hand and foot, and I'll do it. Maybe next week I'd come out to see how you're getting along, but I might forget."

Moorhouse started toward him. Shanaghy kicked his feet out of the stirrups and dropped to the ground. He moved so quickly, Moorhouse was surprised. The big man stopped abruptly, half turned and Tom Shanaghy hit him.

The punch was a good one and Shanaghy could hit, but Moorhouse didn't even stagger. He swung a wicked roundhouse blow that Shanaghy went under, smashing both hands to the ribs.

Moorhouse grabbed him by the shirt and vest and swung him around, throwing him to the ground a half dozen feet away. Tom lit on hands and knees and drove at Moorhouse with a driving tackle that brought the big man crashing down.

Shanaghy was up first. "Get up, Mr. Moorhouse. They

tell me you're a tough man. You can let me search the place or continue with this nonsense and take a beating."

"Nobody ever beat me," Moorhouse said, and he started at Shanaghy.

Tom feinted and smashed a right to the ribs. He stepped around, feinted again and started the right. Moorhouse rushed, swinging with both fists. He caught Tom with a roundhouse left that knocked him staggering, and followed it up with a clubbing right that drove him to his knees. Tom came up fast, hooking to the body again, and Moorhouse grabbed him in his huge hands, throwing him over his knee. "Now I break your back," he said calmly.

Shanaghy turned, twisted and tried to break free, but the big hands drove him back. Excruciating pain shot through Tom's back. He jerked a hand free and smashed a right to the big man's face. He seemed impervious to blows, as Tom hammered him again and again, and then he hunched himself higher and began to press Shanaghy down harder and harder.

Shanaghy threw his legs high, trying to break free, then higher. He managed to lock one leg under Moorhouse's chin and against his throat.

He smashed his knee toward the man's Adam's apple. Although he did not reach it, the big man let go with one hand to tear the leg from his throat. Shanaghy gave a terrific lunge and broke free.

He staggered to his feet and Moorhouse came up, diving at him. Shanaghy clubbed him behind the head, driving him to the earth. Moorhouse came up again, caught him with a wild swing, and Shanaghy stepped inside, ripping wicked uppercuts to the bigger man's unprotected body. Moorhouse staggered and went back, and Tom threw a high overhand right to the chin.

It caught Moorhouse squarely and he went to his knees.

Tom Shanaghy backed off a step. "Get up," he said. "You wanted to fight. Now let's get started."

Moorhouse looked at his bruised knuckles. "There has been enough fighting for today," he said sourly.

"Then I shall search the house."

"Search and be damned. There is nothing there." Moorhouse turned and stared at him from bloody, battered features. "They have beaten you," he said. "You are whipped."

He smiled, revealing a broken tooth and bloody lips. "And now they will kill you. I heard them say it. If it is the last thing they do, they will kill you."

# Chapter XIX

A quick survey of the house revealed nothing beyond the fact that a woman had been living there. A few odds and ends remained, a broken comb for her hair, some strands of ash-blonde hair, and a faint lingering perfume, almost intangible.

Moorhouse was sitting on the steps, his head in his hands, when Shanaghy emerged. He looked up, a bloody handkerchief in his hands. "You hit hard," he said grudgingly.

"You asked for it."

"That I did. Never figgered anybody could do it."

"No need to feel ashamed. I've done some bare-knuckle fighting."

"Figgered it. Why I quit. There's no use bucking a stacked deck."

Shanaghy sat down beside him. "These folks friends of yours?"

"Not by a damn sight. That woman . . . She's too high an' mighty. Ordered me around like I was a slave. Only one she'd talk to was him."

"Holstrum?"

"Aye. Seems like she'd set her cap for him—only I don't think she liked him, either. They was up to something, all of them together."

"They stole a gold shipment that was to pay off cowhands in town. Most of it belonged to Greenwood."

The big man was silent, dabbing at his broken mouth. "Well, I done killed a man or two but I'm no thief. I'd no part in it."

"Didn't think you had. How many of them are there?"

"There's him . . . Holstrum, I mean, and there's that young woman who lived here. Then there was George Alcott, Pin Brodie, an' there was two others whose names

156

I never did get. They didn't come here but once or twice."

"They are all together now?"

"They are."

"Any idea where they are headed?"

"You think they'd talk to me? Scarce give me the time of day. Was I you I'd guess they was going east. Two or three of them are easterners, and her who was running the shebang, she wanted to go east."

"The woman who lived here? She was running the show?"

"Not her. The other woman. I never seen her. She come here a couple of times but at night. Seems like she met them out on the grass somewheres. Now and again I heard talk. Led me to thinkin' she was the bull o' the woods . . . the boss, I mean. She was somewheres over west, I reckon. She come and went from that direction, and from a thing or two she said I figgered she had her a place over yonder."

Shanaghy took his time thinking about it. They were on horseback now, and they were headed south, but he had a hunch that Moorhouse's comment was probably the right one, and that they were headed east.

Holstrum had been looking for a "lady," an eastern woman who had what he considered class. Now he had her, and he would have money and he would be heading east. At least, that was the way he had it planned.

"You liked Holstrum?"

Moorhouse shrugged. "He paid me on time. He never complained none. He just wanted folks kept off and away, especially after that woman come. He didn't want anybody around . . . Not that anybody ever did come."

"I think they mean to kill him."

"What?" Moorhouse passed a hand over his brow. "Well, I feared for it. It was plain to see he figgered he was in charge, but he wasn't. Not a'tall. It was that woman, and after her it was George. Holstrum, he give orders an' ever'body was almighty respectful of him, but behind his back they made their own plans. I heared 'em."

The whole gang was riding now and they had a good start. Shanaghy had taken time looking for wagon tracks, and he had lost time in his fight with Moorhouse, but from the information he might save time. Never one to arrive at decisions too quickly, he thought the situation over carefully.

"Mr. Moorhouse? What's off to the south?"

"Ain't nothing. Not for miles 'n miles. Nothing but prairie grass an' antelope. 'Casional buffalo. That's why I figgered east. West there's nothing, either, 'cept maybe that
other woman's place, an' it don't seem likely she'd take 'em
there, her bein' so careful not to be seen, and all."

East, then. Shanaghy thought of it carefully. Holstrum
was known in Kansas City, at least to a few people. If
Shanaghy rode after them, he would have to almost kill
his horse in catching up, and they might have fresh
horses waiting, which would leave him stranded on the
prairie and out of action.

He got up. "Sit tight, Mr. Moorhouse. I'll be calling
on you."

"I ain't arrested?"

Shanaghy grinned and held out his hand. "You're too
good a man to lie in jail. Besides, you've already been
helpful."

"Well . . . Like I say, I killed a man or two but I'm no
thief. My ma raised me better."

Tom Shanaghy stepped into the saddle. His knuckles
were battered and sore and his shirt was torn. He turned
his horse and rode back to town.

All was quiet when he rode in. He stepped down at the
livery stable and saw Greenwood come out of his saloon
and lean on the rail. Judge McBane joined him there.

Leaving the horse, Shanaghy walked slowly down the
street. Greenwood glanced at his torn shirt. "Looks like
you've had some trouble."

"I could use a beer."

"What happened?"

"Moorhouse didn't want to talk. We went around and
around a bit. Then he talked. He's not a bad man."

"They got the gold," Greenwood said. "They said it was
picked up outside of town by somebody with an order
for it. The order was signed by Holstrum and by Carpenter."

"Carpenter? He's dead."

"So he is, but how could the express messenger know
that?"

Shanaghy accepted the beer and took off his derby and
placed it on the bar beside him. Greenwood's news
was no more than what he had expected.

"Did the engineer come in here?"

"Him? Why should he? That train stopped only a few minutes and then pulled out. Seemed like they were glad to get away from here."

Nobody said anything for a minute or two. Shanaghy tasted the beer. He was very dry. The beer was cold and it tasted good.

"Drako's dead, and so are his boys," McBane said. "You shoot almighty straight, son."

"I had to. I wasn't going to get any second chance." Shanaghy drank from his glass. "But I had some help, and I've had no chance to thank them."

"Josh had his own score to settle."

"That's right. Win Drako was about to hang him, one time." Tom straightened up. "Is Dick Pendleton still in town?"

"Matter of fact, he isn't. Josh told him you were in trouble and he came in to help. He rode back to the ranch, in something of a hurry, I guess."

"And Josh? I could use him." He finished his beer. "Thanks, Greenie. I needed that."

"Well, you tried." Greenwood rested his hands on the bar. "Have another beer if you like. Might as well enjoy it. I'm cleaned out."

"I don't think so," Shanaghy said quietly. "I don't think so at all."

Startled, Greenwood stared at him.

Shanaghy was smiling. "I may be guessing all wrong, but I don't think I am. If I am, you may have lost all you say, but if I'm right—"

"If you're right . . . then what?"

"We'll get it all back." Shanaghy hitched his gunbelt into an easier position on his hips. "Is Holstrum around?"

"He closed up when the shooting started. Holstrum never did like gunfire. He'll be around when things look quiet again. Believe me, this isn't the first time Holstrum closed up. At the first sign of trouble he hunts cover."

Tom Shanaghy was thinking about Jan. Dick had ridden out of town in a hurry . . . Why? He had not seen Jan since he left her with Coonskin.

He turned to Judge McBane. "Do you know a man named Coonskin Adams?"

McBane smiled, his eyes twinkling. "Don't tell me you've run into him!"

"Met him."

"Didn't know ol' Coonskin was still around. He's a wolf-hunter. Used to trap the Rockies for fur, then worked for a couple of cow outfits cleaning up the predators."

"Where's he live?"

McBane chuckled. "Now *that's* a question! To tell you the truth, I doubt if anybody has ever asked that question. Coonskin is one of those people you see around. He comes and he goes. He's here one day, gone the next. He's not a man who talks of himself even when he is around."

"Somebody killed his burro," Shanaghy said.

McBane's expression changed. "God help them then."

"I need to talk to him."

"Go where you last saw him and build yourself a fire. Send up a smoke. Coonskin is as curious as any wild animal, and my bet is he will come to you. McAuliffe, who is division superintendent, knows him well and he might give you a lead. Send him a wire."

McAuliffe . . . Big Mac? Maybe.

"Judge? Do the folks here still think I killed Carpenter?"

"I am afraid they do. I'd heard the story before ever I got down to breakfast, told me as the gospel. I must say I never believed it for a moment."

The door opened and Josh Lundy came in. His rifle was cradled on his arm. "Heard you was back. They got away?"

"Not yet."

Lundy looked at him carefully. "You got some idea? If I can help, count me in."

"You have helped, but I do need you. I'm going to need some more help."

"I'll come," Greenwood said.

"And I," Judge McBane added. "What have you got in mind?"

Briefly, Shanaghy explained how the train had been deliberately backed in front of him to block pursuit, then described his arrival at Holstrum's place, and what he had learned from Moorhouse.

"Judge, I want authority from you to search Holstrum's store and his living quarters. If he is there, then at least part of my conclusions are wrong, but I am betting that he's gone. And then," he added, "I want us all at the depot to take the evening train east."

McBane shook his head. "Shanaghy, I can't permit you to enter a man's private premises on nothing but suspicion."

"Suppose we go knock on his door? If he answers the door I shall go no further with it. If he doesn't, I want to search the area . . . if I have to," he added. "I shall do it on my own authority." He smiled. "If I am wrong you can please the town by firing me."

"I can't believe Holstrum is involved," McBane said.

"Judge, he is a man with a dream. He's a great, hulking, somewhat near-sighted man, but all his life he has dreamed of young, sophisticated women. Suddenly such a woman is here, and he believes she is going to be his. He believes the money is the key to it."

"Do you mean he planned it all?" asked the judge.

Shanaghy shrugged. "I doubt it. He may have started it or somebody may sort of suggested it . . . Not right out, maybe. I don't know how it all happened. I don't even know if I am right, but we're going to find out."

He turned to the door. "Judge? If you'd like to come? And Josh?"

Tom Shanaghy went up the few steps to the store's walk. His footsteps echoed hollowly as he walked along, followed by McBane and Josh. He paused at the store's door. There was a sign: CLOSED UNTIL FURTHER NOTICE.

"Same sign he always uses," Josh commented.

Tom rapped on the door, and the sound echoed hollowly. He waited, listening. When there was no sound, he rapped again.

"His living quarters are in the back. There's a door around to the side."

Again Shanaghy led the way. There was a sinking inside him. Secretly he had been hoping he would find Holstrum within. He wanted to find no man guilty, and even though all pointed to Holstrum, he could be wrong. He hoped he was wrong. He knew how a dream could die, and how futile had been the dreams of this man. How much worse it would have been for him had he realized the dream in fact, for what could two such people have said to each other? What could they have done together? Sometimes it was better to keep the dream and forget the realization.

Shanaghy rapped on the back door, and there was no

response. Josh walked back to the stable. "His horse is gone," he called.

Shanaghy took hold of the doorknob, hesitated. For he shrank at entering the home of another, uninvited. Yet he put his shoulder to the door and the foolish lock burst.

There was a bare, simple room. A rag rug on the floor, plus two chairs and an old leather settee. There were two paintings on the wall, mystic, ethereal things . . . obviously originals, like something Poe might have visioned.

There were a few books, several of poetry, but only the first few leaves had been cut as if the reader had gone that far and stopped. There were a bottle of whiskey and a glass, the bottle half empty. There was a bottle of Chateau LaFite with one drink gone.

The bed was made, neatly tucked in. The few clothes in the closet were nicely hung. The drawers were half closed as if Holstrum had packed in a hurry.

The drawers were empty except for one. There was a dainty handkerchief edged with lace . . . perhaps a memento of the girl Holstrum had seen but once and then never again. Shanaghy picked it up, glanced at it and dropped it back into the drawer. He remembered something Holstrum had said, or that had been said about him, about looking in a window and seeing some elegantly clad people dancing. Well, Holstrum was still looking in windows, and he was still standing outside.

Shanaghy swore softly, and McBane glanced at him. "He's missed the boat again," Tom said, "I wish he could have made it, just once."

"You have compassion, my friend. One does not often find it in an officer."

"More often than you think," Shanaghy said.

"And maybe Holstrum will make it this time."

"No . . ." Shanaghy shook his head slowly. "I know the kind of people he is dealing with and he does not. He is thinking of her, and of what they can do in some great city. She is thinking of that money, and what she can do. And George is thinking of the money and wondering how he can wind up with all or most of it. And I think that other man, I think he is the one named McBride. I think he intends to have it all and knows how he will . . . And they are all wrong unless I can stop something here."

"Here?"

"We must get our tickets."

Shanaghy closed the door behind him, fastening it as securely as possible. They walked back up the alley together. A few people were in the streets now, and some were talking, pointing out where the men had stood when the gunfight took place.

Shanaghy paused. "You said . . . I killed them?"

"Both," Josh said, "dead center. I never did see better shootin'. Wilson Drako was here on the steps. He went down right there, and Dandy, who was clerkin' at the ho-tel . . ."

"The clerk was a Drako? The one with the rifle?"

"Didn't you know? Sure, he was a Drako, and he hated your guts."

They had paused on the boardwalk in front of Greenwood's saloon. "Judge, Josh . . . where we're going isn't far, I'm thinking. But at the end of it there will be shooting, and when there's that much money at stake they won't care who they kill, or how many."

"I cut my teeth on a shootin' iron," the judge said dryly. "I fit Injuns before I was dry behind the ears, and I served four years in the War Between the States. I can stand beside any man when it comes to gunfire."

"All right." Shanaghy paused. "Judge, we're going to take that evening train out. Josh, you go down and get the tickets for us. Don't mention where we're going, just buy tickets for Kansas City."

Shanaghy took the money from his pocket. "And above all, don't tell that agent or anybody else who's going along. If you want, tell them it's for the Pendletons."

"Do you think he's in on this?" McBane asked.

"I do."

"And that engineer? And the brakeman?"

"I think they were slipped a few dollars just to act stupid with the train. And, if anybody came along, to block the road.

"They had it all timed nicely. I think they had practiced taking that wagon down, and I believe they had horses waiting. And I think they ran them hard to the Holstrum place and then took off on fresh stock.

"By now they are swinging back around to meet the railroad line—"

"What if they don't?"

"Then I'll have my work cut out for me. But look at it this way. Some of these people are easterners. The railroad is something they know. They'd have to ride a long, long way to get anywhere a'horseback. They won't have any idea we have this figured out, and they'll think we're running in circles back here. When that train pulls in and they want to board it, we'll be waiting for them. With luck we can do it without shooting . . . but don't bank on it."

It was a long shot, and he knew it. Shanaghy checked his guns, then reholstered them.

"Judge"—he saw Josh coming back up the street with the tickets—"there's one more thing. Maybe I've read this right and maybe I haven't. Somebody said once, 'Set a crook to catch a crook.' Well, I'm no thief but I've known a'plenty of them back in New York town. I think what we've got here is one of the nastiest triple-crosses I've ever seen."

"We'd better get on down to the station," Greenwood suggested.

"Wait . . . we'll hear the whistle and we can start then. It's less than a hundred yards.

"What's happening must have started just about the time you people got together and planned to bring money in here to pay off the cattle drivers, and I don't know whose idea it was . . . Maybe it started in two or three places, but I do know there's one person who not only wanted *all* the money, but was a bitter, vengeful person along with it.

"They think they've won. They have the money, or think they do, and only one thing remains. That's to kill the man who caused them so much trouble, and somebody has figured out a way of doing it without risk."

"Without risk? *You?*" Josh exclaimed. "That's crazy! Why, I've seen you in action and there isn't a man—"

"That's right," Shanaghy said quietly, "so . . ."

Mrs. Carpenter was walking up the street toward them.

# Chapter XX

She was neatly dressed in a fashionable black traveling dress, with a small bonnet perched on her head. In her hand she carried a handbag.

"You've got to be crazy!" Greenwood said. "Why—!"

"The story is around that I killed her husband. She is a bereaved wife. Who else could kill a man, in this country, and get away with it? Even have the blessing of most of the townspeople?"

"You mean she was in on it?"

"Maybe not from the beginning, but you can just bet most of the planning was hers. And right now, if she kills me, she can board that train and ride off a wealthy woman, sharing with no one but her brother."

"But they have the gold!"

"Maybe, but I doubt it. I don't believe the gold ever left the train."

She was walking up to them now and she had slipped her hand inside her bag. She stopped. Her thin, rather pretty face was drawn in suddenly hard lines.

"Marshal, you are an evil man! You murdered my husband! You killed him and then tried to burn the—"

"Mrs. Carpenter," Shanaghy said. "Sure, ma'am, and you're too late. It's all over. We know what was done and how it was done, and we know that you yourself killed your husband, and that it was you who closed the doors and set the barn afire.

"It was you, with your brother, who planned to steal all that gold."

Her eyes tightened at the corners, as did her mouth. "I have no idea what you are talking about, and—"

"Mrs. Carpenter, I have no desire to be rough with a woman—even one who has murdered her husband and probably others as well. So please . . . Do not try to take that gun from your purse, because I—"

Her hand started to come out from the handbag, but almost casually Shanaghy slapped the purse from her hand with his left and then brought his right hand up under the barrel, twisting it up and away. It was let go or have a broken finger, and Mrs. Carpenter let go. Shanaghy passed the gun to Judge McBane.

"It is all over, Mrs. Carpenter, all over. None of it worked."

She was very cool. The hardness became only a shadow in her eyes, covered by amused contempt. "You're such a *little* man, Marshal, so pleased with yourself, taking a gun away from a woman. Mr. Holstrum will testify—"

"Holstrum is dead," Shanaghy said.

McBane turned his head sharply and Josh was staring.

"Or if he is not, I shall be very surprised. You see, Mrs. Carpenter, some of the others were thinking just as you were. Once outside of town Holstrum was no longer needed, so why share with him? I am betting they killed him somewhere between his ranch and that little station thirty miles east where they planned to rejoin the train." He smiled. "Rejoin it with what they thought was the gold."

"You mean they don't have it?" Greenwood exclaimed.

"As I said, it never left the train. What they took off at the water tank were some boxes prepared for the purpose. Mrs. Carpenter's brother, as station agent, had connived to get the manifest changed. The boxes that actually contained the money were being shipped right back to Kansas City . . . where Mrs. Carpenter would pick them up."

"You mean they have already been shipped back?"

"My guess is that they went west last night, and that they will be on the evening train when we board it."

Mrs. Carpenter stood stock-still, her hands clasping her purse, staring off into space. Yet, while there might be some shock at being frustrated, at having all her carefully laid plans go sky-high, Shanaghy had an idea her mind was working swiftly toward some sort of a solution.

"I'd like to go home now," she said suddenly.

Shanaghy shook his head. "You're not thinking clearly, Mrs. Carpenter. You are under arrest. But something which you should be thinking of now is your friends, if you can call them that."

She merely looked at him.

"If they have not already discovered that they do not have the gold, they will discover it very soon. They will also suspect what has happened, and when they do I would imagine they would be looking for you.

"Of course, your plans were to be on the train going east by now, and so safely away. But you are not going east, and neither are they."

He paused. "So I shall lock you up until we return."

She looked her contempt. "Will you shackle me to the hitching-rail as you did those others?"

He shook his head. "No, Mrs. Carpenter. Holstrum has a storeroom where we can leave you until we return, which will not be long."

In the distance, a train whistled. "Greenwood, would you lock her up? And stay here, if you will. Vince Patterson and his boys should be riding in today and they will want some drinks. Get hold of Vince and tell him what has happened. Tell him everything."

They walked to the station. The train whistled again, still far off. Josh reached into his pocket. "By the way, this letter was in your box at the ho-tel. I seen it there after we checked the clerk's body . . . You know, Dandy Drako? I figured you'd be wantin' it."

Shanaghy glanced at it. He recognized the handwriting. The letter was from John Morrissey. But there was no time to read it now. That could wait for a more leisurely time. He put the letter in his shirt pocket.

For the first time he took a look at himself. His shirt was badly torn. His face felt stiff and sore from several punches he had taken. He did not even remember them. You never did, at times like that, except maybe the very hard ones.

The train was coming down the track and the agent came out to the platform. He looked at them, stopped and started to go back inside.

"Don't do it," Shanaghy said in a conversational tone of voice.

The agent looked at him. His tongue touched his lips. He was trying to make up his mind, and Tom Shanaghy was remembering that the man had a gun . . . probably back inside.

"He means it, Burt," Josh Lundy said. "If I were you I wouldn't try."

"What's wrong? I don't know what's going on."

"You just come with us. You'll learn."

"Come with you? Leave my post, here? I can't do that, and you can't make me. I—"

"You won't be gone long, not this time." Shanaghy smiled. "Someday we will have to sit down and you can tell me about your sister. She's an interesting lady."

"Helen? You mean Mrs. Carpenter?"

"I do."

"I've no idea what you're talking about, Marshal. Look, I've got to go in there and clear some messages and also let them know this train's gone through."

"Later. Right now we're just going down the track a little ways to meet some of your friends. If they haven't discovered the double-cross you two have pulled off, they'll be wanting to load those boxes off the pack animals they have. If they have discovered the cross, they'll be hunting you and your sister."

Burt's face had taken on a sickly expression. "Marshal, I don't know what you're talking about."

"You do know." Shanaghy watched the train pull in. "Search him and take him aboard," he told Josh. "I'll just walk along and check the engineer."

The engineer was a different man from before, a burly fellow with white hair and a florid face.

"My name is Shanaghy," Tom said, "and I'm marshal here. There's been a little trouble and some of us are going to ride down the track with you. About thirty miles down the track, there will be some men waiting at that little way station, some men and probably one woman. Stop the train and then get down on the floor. There may be a little lead flying."

Once seated on the train, Shanaghy looked over at Josh. "Tell me what you see as we come up to the station," he suggested. "I want to have a little talk with Burt, here." Tom glanced over at Judge McBane. "Judge? Would you like to join me? Maybe if we can ask this man the right questions we can keep him alive."

"Keep me alive?" Burt started up and Shanaghy pushed him back down into his seat. "What do you mean?"

Shanaghy smiled. "Now, see here! You and your sister

double-crossed your partners. You don't expect them to
like it, do you? You've been playing with some pretty
rough company, Burt, and now that the bottom has
fallen out of your plans, they are going to think it was
you . . . they will know it was you.

"They will be waiting at the station right ahead of us,
but if you talk fast and give us everything you know we
may be able to save you."

"I don't need to be saved!" Burt protested. "I've nothing to—"

"Then you won't mind getting off at the next station
to meet George and Pin? They'll be there, you know."

"The train's not stopping," Burt protested. "You can't
pull that on me. I sent the orders."

"Of course, you did. I just changed them. I know that
you and your sister expected to be on this train, and
you expected it to fly right by, leaving your old friends
standing on the platform. That was the idea, wasn't it?
You'd have the gold and they would just have several
small but heavy boxes.

"Well, that isn't the way it's going to happen. We are
going to stop there, but just long enough to put you off."

Burt was sweating, his brow was beaded with it. His
face had taken on an even more sickly look, and his eyes
seemed unusually large. "Marshal, you can't do that! You
can't put me off! Why, that would be murder!"

"Like what your sister Helen did to her husband, you
mean? Like what your associates have done with Holstrum?"

"Holstrum? He's dead?"

"Well, we don't know, but he left with them and with
that woman he was sweet on, but I'm betting they decided once they had the loot that they didn't need him
any more. I hope I'm wrong. But you know how it is.
They'll be thinking just like your sister and you . . . who
wanted it all."

"Where is she?"

"We have her . . ." Shanaghy took out his big silver
watch. "Well, it won't be long now. Josh, you see anything yet?"

"Too soon."

Shanaghy got up. "Judge, talk to this man, will you?
We've got maybe twenty miles to go, and if he doesn't

tell us anything by the time we get there I'm going to just drop him off at the next station. You talk some sense into him if you can while I go along up to the baggage car."

Only three passengers rode in the only other passenger car and Shanaghy walked through, opening the door into the baggage car.

The express-man looked startled when Shanaghy walked in, then relieved when he glimpsed the badge. "Something I can do for you, Officer?"

Shanaghy glanced around, unsure of what to look for beyond an approximate capacity. "Your heaviest shipment," he said, "I'd like to see that."

"Heaviest?" the express-man looked thoughtful. "We have several heavy ones. Right there"—he indicated several solidly built boxes—"those are the heaviest ones."

"Where were they loaded?"

He shrugged. "They were here when I took over from the other man," he said. He glanced at the labels tied on the boxes. "Kansas City," he said, "to H. R. Carpenter. It's stenciled on the boxes, too."

"It's a stolen shipment," Shanaghy said. "If you check your records you will see that such a shipment was directed to Greenwood, Holstrum & Carpenter yesterday. The weights will be the same."

"You taking this one?"

"We are, in the name of the above parties. I will sign for it. Judge McBane is with me."

"I don't know whether I can do that, Marshal. Maybe we—"

"Leave it to us. And one more thing, when the train stops don't open your doors under any circumstances. If I were you I'd lie down on the floor behind those boxes and stay there until we pull out of the station."

"There'll be shooting?"

"Unless I miss my guess there will be some, but we will be doing our share."

The train was slowing. Swiftly, Shanaghy ran back through the cars.

Josh was at the door with a Winchester. There was another man beside him. "This here's Joel Strong. He was on the train, and when he found what was happening he wanted a piece of the action."

"I remember him. He was speaking to the judge here on my first morning in town. All right, consider yourself a deputy."

He walked over to McBane. "Well, Burt," he said, "have you anything to say?"

"He's said it," McBane replied. "We have all we need."

The train was slowing down for its stop at the station. Shanaghy took his gun from the holster and checked the chambers once more. Then the other gun.

George . . . George would be good with a gun, he knew that. Pin McBride would, also. McBride was the man who made him jump from the moving train. If it could be done without shooting, well and good . . . But Shanaghy did not believe it could.

McBane stood beside him. "It began with Greenwood and Holstrum when they went to Kansas City to arrange for the shipment of gold. The blonde woman, I do not have her name straight, was at dinner with friends, and she heard of these men who had come into the bank, and of the gold shipment they had arranged. She was a girl who had once been wealthy and wanted to be again, and the idea came to her. She had seen George a time or two, knew he was a gambler and worse, and she got the hostler in a stable to bring him to her.

"She's a very cold, assured young woman," McBane said. "She apparently knew exactly what she was about and believed she could take care of herself. Deliberately, she arranged to meet Holstrum and played up to him. She agreed to come to his town and see it, and when she arrived there she began at once to talk of the pleasant places in Chicago and New York, and what could be done if they only had the money.

"She kept Holstrum at arm's length, and that made him admire her all the more. It seems to have been painfully easy to win him over. He had told her she must not come to town when the money arrived because Vince Patterson and his men might actually try to burn the town.

"It was she who suggested that somebody might take that chance to steal the money . . . and who would know the difference? She had George standing by and he had recruited McBride and the others.

"Mrs. Carpenter had heard of the shipment from her husband. Some of the money, but only a small amount, would be his. By this time she wanted no more of Carpenter or the town.

"She had seen the blonde woman in town, and she had seen George in deep conversation with Holstrum, and she was no fool. She is a woman who trusts no one, who suspects everyone. Knowing about the shipment she became suspicious. She talked to Burt about the gold, when it would arrive and what would be done with it. How long it would be on the platform, and if it were stolen how the thieves could get away with it.

"Burt was scared. But she kept after him. She kept after him with her questions and asked, finally, why the gold had to leave the train at all? If they were going to steal it, why not just change the delivery directions and reship it? And the more he thought of it, the better it looked.

"Burt swears he wouldn't have gone into it at all but for the fact that he started thinking about the others stealing it, if that was what was planned. Unloading at the water tank at Holstrum had not occurred to him, and he got the idea that if they stole it they would have to kill him."

Tom Shanaghy walked to the door of the car. The station ahead was only a boxcar dismounted from its wheels, with a plank platform in front of it. He could see several horses with saddles and others with pack-saddles.

There was only one man in sight, standing alone on the platform. Beside him were several boxes, stacked neatly. Evidently they had not discovered they had been tricked. The man moved forward as the train came to a stop.

"Open up!" he shouted. "We've got some express!"

Nothing happened. Impatiently, he stepped closer. "Hey, in there! Open up!"

Tom Shanaghy glanced at the freight car. Only one man could come out of that door at once, and he saw but one window.

"Josh," he said over his shoulder, "if shooting starts put a bullet through that window."

He stepped down on the platform. "Something I can do for you?" he asked.

Sunlight struck the badge and the man went for his gun. Instantly, another man loomed in the door. It was George Alcott.

Shanaghy drew and fired in the same instant, shooting

at George, whom he suspected of being the best shot. He fired, a second time, at the man beside the boxes.

Josh dropped to the platform, shooting into the window. There was a cry from within, and as quickly as it had begun it was over.

George was down in the doorway. The man beside the boxes was clutching a bloody arm, his gun on the platform at his feet.

Tom Shanaghy walked toward the door and said, "All of you inside there, step outside, hands in the air."

There was a moment of hesitation and then Shanaghy said, just loud enough, "If you imagine those walls are shelter, let me tell you this. A forty-four or forty-five bullet will go through six inches of pine . . . You've got about an inch. Come out, hands up, or we are going to shoot that car so full of holes it will look like a sieve."

They came out—another stranger first, then the girl, and lastly, Pin McBride.

"Where's Holstrum?" he asked.

Nobody said anything. The blonde girl's face was drawn and her lips were compressed. She was staring at him, frightened and angry.

As she stepped around George's body, she shrank from him, holding her skirts away. She did not look at the man seated on the boxes. He was holding his wounded arm and cursing in a low, monotonous voice.

Shanaghy walked to McBride and took a pistol from him. McBride glared at him. "Damn you! I should have killed you!"

"You might have," Shanaghy replied, "makin' me jump that way. If it will give you any pleasure, you might as well know that making me jump off that train and then throwing that gear after me was what blew up your show."

"What d'you mean?"

"First, you made me mad. Second, those duds you threw after me belonged to Rig Barrett. His guns were in the bed-roll." He smiled. "You see? It was your own pigheaded attitude that brought you to this."

The girl's eyes were furious. "Just what do you think you're doing?" she demanded. "I was just waiting for the train—!"

"Good!" He smiled at her. "Because it's right here, waiting for you. Before we put you aboard, we'd better have a look at these nice little boxes you have here.

"Now, these boxes should contain about twelve thousand twenty-dollar gold pieces, and about ten thousand dollars in silver."

From the engineer Shanaghy borrowed a hammer and knocked loose a couple of boards. He lifted the boards and tore loose the sacking inside the boxes.

"All of you . . . have a look."

McBride swung around, angrily. "You don't have to show me . . . !" His voice broke off and he stared, his face slowly turning pale.

The boxes were filled with nuts, bolts and screws.

# Chapter XXI

At his expression the blonde girl turned her head. When she saw the boxes Shanaghy thought for a moment she was going to cry. Then her face took on a hard, ugly look.

"The trouble with being a crook," Shanaghy said mildly, "is that you have to associate with so many dishonest people."

"Who did that?" McBride demanded. "How the devil—?"

"Looks like you boys have been played for suckers," Shanaghy continued. He turned to Josh. "You an' Joel hogtie this lot, including the lady. If you take my advice you'll watch her most of all."

She kept glancing at the train, and clutching her handbag in her left hand. He reached over and took the handbag from her. She started to pull it away but he took it with a quick jerk. When he opened it he found a .44 Derringer in it. He showed it to Joel Strong and Josh. "Can't be too careful," he added.

"What happened to that gold?" McBride demanded.

"If it gets into the papers, you can read about it there," Shanaghy said. He turned to Josh. "Take 'em aboard now."

"Where are we going?" Judge McBane asked from the doorway.

"Back to town," he said. "I'll speak to the engineer."

The train started to back up the track. Shanaghy walked forward to the express car. When he opened the door the express messenger shook his head. "Man, they had me running scared there, for a minute, with that shootin' and all."

"Don't let it worry you. I think it's all over."

He glanced at the shipment, then walked back to the car where the prisoners rode. Despite their mild objections, McBane had moved the other passengers into the other coach, so they had the prisoners and themselves in the car alone.

Josh had taken a seat at one end of the car facing the prisoners, and Joel Strong at the other. Two of the prisoners were seated together. McBride sat alone as did the girl.

Shanaghy was tired. He was feeling the letdown from days of thinking and worry. He paused by McBride. "Are you the one who shot an old prospector's burro out by the water tank?"

McBride looked up. "You going to arrest me for that, too?"

"No," Shanaghy said. "I think with trying to steal the gold shipment and the murder of Holstrum, we've got enough on you. Then there's the attack on Rig Barrett, resisting an officer and a good deal more. Take my advice, though. If you get a chance to escape, don't take it."

"What's that mean?"

"That old man whose burro you killed. He'd like nothing better than to get a shot at you. And if you do escape I am not even going to look for you. He'll take care of it."

"That old blister? Hell, I should've shot him as well as his burro."

"Well, you didn't, and that's a mighty hard old man. And he loved that burro. He's taking it mighty bad."

Greenwood was at the station when the train backed in and he watched the prisoners get off. He also watched the body of George taken from the train.

"Holstrum?" he asked.

"I think they killed him. They aren't talking about him, so I'll have to ride out that way and have a look. Anyway, he didn't show up here."

Shanaghy himself helped unload the boxes containing the gold. "There it is, Greenie," he said. "Now you can supply the money to pay off those cowhands."

Greenwood looked at the boxes and shook his head. "Tom, I'm damned if I know what to say. You've saved the town and our money, too, and mighty poor treatment you've had for it."

"Fix me up with a room at the hotel again, and I'll ask for nothing more."

"No problem. They all know who killed Carp now, and most of them are sorry for the way they acted." He paused. "By the way, you've some friends in town . . . at least they were asking for you."

"Friends? I don't know anybody in this part of the country."

Greenwood lit a cigar. "Don't appear to be from around here. I'd say they were easterners. There's four of them."

Easterners? Who— Suddenly he remembered the letter from John Morrissey. He felt in his pockets for it, then opened it.

*Dear Tom:*

*No need for you to come back unless you wish to. What you started when you left worked out fine and the Childers people are gone . . . cleaned out. However, if I were in your boots I would keep a sharp eye out. The Childers are still around and you were the one they wanted most of all.*

*Lochlin is well, and sends regards.*

*My advice is stay west. You are too good a man for this, and you could make a place for yourself in that new country like I did when I landed in New York.*

The letter was signed with a flourish, *John Morrissey.*

Greenwood was watching him as he read. "What is it? Bad news?"

Shanaghy folded the letter and put it in his pocket. The Childers family had come from someplace in the west or midwest, and so might know this country. Finding him would not be difficult, especially if they had somebody keeping an eye on Morrissey's mail. This letter was probably written the same day Morrissey received his note. Even without that, there were only two rail lines into the west and this was the logical one.

"It could be trouble," he admitted. "Those men you spoke of could be some old enemies, from New York."

His eyes on the street, he explained, briefly. The thoroughfare was busy now, the people coming and going about their shopping, for this was a Saturday, always a big day in town.

"If it's who I think it is," Shanaghy said, "this is my affair. They are hunting me and nobody else."

"You're our town marshal," Greenwood objected, gently. "And we don't like outsiders meddling in our affairs." He grinned. "Meaning no offense."

"You know," Shanaghy said, "the only one of them I have any sympathy for is Holstrum. He had a dream. Maybe it was foolish, maybe not. Seems that was all he wanted from life."

"We'll miss Carp. He was a good man."

"Aye," Shanaghy was watching the hotel. Where were they? Did they know he was back in town? He looked around, taking his time.

Judge McBane walked over. "We've locked up your prisoners. That young woman wants to talk to you."

"All right." He walked away, following Strong.

She had been locked in another storeroom at Holstrum's, the place where he kept sacks of flour, sugar, and seed. It was a temporary place at best.

She was sitting up when he came into the room, and she got quickly to her feet. "Marshal, you can help me. I've got to get out of this!"

"What do you mean?"

"All this. I never intended . . . I mean I never meant for this to happen! It's impossible! I mean, my family, my friends—"

"You should have thought of that before."

"How could I? I never expected—"

"You never expected to get caught, is that it? You never expected to have to go to prison, to have a trial, to be in court as a person on trial for robbery and murder."

"*Murder?*" she gasped. "You can't believe I had anything to do with *that!*"

"You started it all, ma'am. You were the instigator, and as such you're the most guilty of all. The truth of the matter is, ma'am, that nobody would commit a crime if they expected to get caught. Every criminal believes he is going to get away with it."

"But I never did anything like this before! Marshal, it was my first offense, and believe me it will be my last. Doesn't that count for anything?"

"I will do as much for you as you will for Holstrum."

"But he's *dead!*"

"That's right, ma'am. So is Mr. Carpenter. All because a greedy, selfish girl wanted more than she had. When you can bring them back to life, ma'am, you come and ask me for help. Every man and woman should consider the consequences of his or her actions, and those actions should be considered beforehand, not after. I've no use for crybabies, ma'am, male or female."

The pleading, woebegone look was gone from her eyes. What Shanaghy saw now was pure hatred, but he wasn't talking any more and he wasn't listening any more.

When he closed the door behind him, he didn't feel any better. Suddenly all he wanted was to be finished with it all. He wanted to sit down to a quiet meal and a cup of coffee, and most of all he wanted to see Jan.

They would be taken east somewhere for trial. No doubt he would be called upon to testify, as would Greenwood, Judge McBane and others. And Burt . . . who had turned state's evidence.

When Shanaghy came out of Holstrum's store, Josh Lundy was standing in front of Greenwood's with Joel Strong and Judge McBane. Greenwood came out as Shanaghy appeared.

All were armed. "What is this?" he asked. "Another war?"

"It could be. Those are Childerses up there. They say they are hunting you."

"Thanks, gentlemen, but that's my problem."

"Not if there's four of them and you're our marshal."

Tom Shanaghy had taken no more than half a dozen steps when there was a rustle of movement and the soft pound of hoofs. Several riders brushed by him. Others came through the intervals between the buildings, slowly converging on the hotel.

He caught a glimpse of the Childers men on the hotel porch, and then they were blocked out by at least twenty riders in the street.

Shanaghy paused, and between the horses he glimpsed the Childers men being escorted toward the station by a dozen riders, all with Winchesters.

One of the other riders turned and rode toward him. It was Red, the Vince Patterson rider he had seen at their chuckwagon. "We're just a'showin' those boys some horsepitality," he said, "guidin' 'em to the *dee*pot, like. We surely can't afford to let a man get shot who offered to stand for drinks for the crowd now, can we?"

"This was my fight," Shanaghy objected.

"What fight?" Red asked, innocently. "Come on, Irishman, keep your derby on. Let's just head back down to that drinkin' establishment I see yonder."

Shanaghy turned and walked back to Greenwood's. He had scarcely reached the bar when Vince Patterson strode in. "Everything all right, Marshal?"

"Sure, everything's all right. Have yourself a drink. As Red here reminded me, I'm standing treat."

"With pleasure." Vince Patterson accepted the drink and then said, "A couple of my boys found the body of your storekeeper a few miles south. We brought it in. He'd been shot in the back of the head at close range."

"It's been a trying time," Shanaghy said, "a most trying time."

"My boys are glad to be here," Vince assured him, "and I am sure they will cause no trouble."

"Red," Shanaghy said, "will you boys hang up your guns here until you leave town?"

Red shrugged. "Looks like we got no choice." He grinned. "I wouldn't want to get mowed down by those *fee*rocious townspeople you got here."

Tom Shanaghy finished his drink and walked outside with Vince.

"Why don't we ride out to the Pendletons?" Vince suggested. "I hear there's a young lady out there who is most anxious to see you. And," he added, "she has a gentleman who is recuperating from some serious wounds, a man named Rig Barrett who would like a firsthand report from a deputy he never heard of."

It was long after dark when Tom Shanaghy rode into town, and Josh Lundy met him in the street. "Pin McBride escaped!" he said. "Somebody got the door open and let him out."

Shanaghy dismounted and handed his horse to Josh. "Put him up, will you? We'll go hunting for his body in the morning."

"Body?"

"Rig Barrett was out at the Pendletons. Jan got Coonskin Adams to help her get him out there to her place, where they could take proper care of him."

"What about Pin?"

"No trouble. I am sure you'll find his body out east of town not far from that water tank. Just look for the carcass of a dead burro. His will be right close by."

# ABOUT THE AUTHOR

LOUIS L'AMOUR, born Louis Dearborn L'Amour, is of French-Irish descent. Although Mr. L'Amour claims his writing began as a "spur-of-the-moment thing," prompted by friends who relished his verbal tales of the West, he comes by his talent honestly. A frontiersman by heritage (his grandfather was scalped by the Sioux), and a universal man by experience, Louis L'Amour lives the life of his fictional heroes. Since leaving his native Jamestown, North Dakota, at the age of fifteen, he's been a longshoreman, lumberjack, elephant handler, hay shocker, flume builder, fruit picker, and an officer on tank destroyers during World War II. And he's written four hundred short stories and over fifty books (including a volume of poetry).

Mr. L'Amour has lectured widely, traveled the West thoroughly, studied archaeology, compiled biographies of over one thousand Western gunfighters, and read prodigiously (his library holds more than two thousand volumes). And he's watched thirty-one of his westerns as movies. He's circled the world on a freighter, mined in the West, sailed a dhow on the Red Sea, been shipwrecked in the West Indies, stranded in the Mojave Desert. He's won fifty-one of fifty-nine fights as a professional boxer and pinch-hit for Dorothy Kilgallen when she was on vacation from her column. Since 1816, thirty-three members of his family have been writers. And, he says, "I could sit in the middle of Sunset Boulevard and write with my typewriter on my knees; temperamental I am not."

Mr. L'Amour is re-creating an 1865 Western town, christened Shalako, where the borders of Utah, Arizona, New Mexico, and Colorado meet. Historically authentic from whistle to well, it will be a live, operating town, as well as a movie location and tourist attraction.

Mr. L'Amour now lives in Los Angeles with his wife Kathy, who helps with the enormous amount of research he does for his books. Soon, Mr. L'Amour hopes, the children (Beau and Angelique) will be helping too.

A Special Preview of
the exciting opening pages of

# BENDIGO SHAFTER

The new novel of the west by
# LOUIS L'AMOUR

# 1

Where the wagons stopped we built our homes, making the cabins tight against the winter's coming. Here in this place we would build our town, here we would create something new.

We would space our buildings, lay out our streets and dig wells to provide water for our people. The idea of it filled me with a heartwarming excitement such as I had not known before.

Was it this feeling of creating something new that held my brother Cain to his forge throughout the long hours? He knew the steel he turned in his hands, knew the weight of the hammer and where to strike, knew by the glow of the iron what its temperature would be; even the leap of the sparks had a message for his experience.

He knew when to heat and when to strike and when to dip the iron into water; yet when is the point at which a group of strangers becomes a community? What it is that forges the will of a people?

This I did not know, nor had I books to advise me, nor any experience to judge a matter of this kind. We who now were alien, strangers drawn together by wagons moving westward, must learn to work together, to fuse our interests, and to become as one. This we must do if we were to survive and become a town.

No settlement lay nearer than Fort Bridger, more than a hundred miles to the southwest . . . or so we had heard.

All about us was Indian country, and we were few.

There were seven men to do the building, two boys to guard our stock, and thirteen women and children to gather wood and buffalo chips for the fires of the nights to come, and kindling against a time of snow.

Only now did we realize that we were strangers, and each looked upon the other with distant eyes, judging and being judged, uneasy and causing uneasiness, for here we had elected to make our stand, and we knew not the temper of those with whom we stood.

It was Ruth Macken, but lately become a widow, who led the move to stop while supplies remained to us, and we who stood beside her were those who favored her decision and joined with her in stopping.

My father had been a Bible-reading man and named his sons from the Book. Four of our brothers had gone the way of flesh, and of the boys only we two remained. Cain, a wedded man with two children, and I, Bendigo Shafter, eighteen and a man with hands to work.

Our sister was with us. Lorna was a pretty sixteen, named for a cousin in Wales.

"You will build for the Widow Macken," Cain said to me. "Her Bud is a man for his twelve years, but young for the lifting of logs and the notching."

So I went up the hill through the frost of the morning, pausing when I reached the bench where their cabin would stand. A fair place it was, with a cold spring spilling its water down to the meadow where our oxen and horses grazed upon the brown grass of autumn. Tall pines, sentinel straight, made a park of the bench, and upon the steep slope behind there was a good stand of timber.

The view from the bench was a fine one, and I stood to look upon it, filling myself with the quiet morning and the beauty of the long valley below the Beaver Rim.

"You have an eye for beauty, Mr. Shafter," Ruth Macken said to me, and I kept my eyes from her, feeling the flush and the heat climbing my neck as it forever did when a pretty woman spoke to me. "It is a good thing in a man."

"It works a magic," I said, "to look upon distance."

"Some people can't abide it. Bigness makes them feel small instead of offering a challenge, but I am glad my Bud will grow to manhood here. A big country can breed big men."

"Yes, ma'am." I glanced about the bench. "I have come to build you a cabin, then."

"Build it so when spring comes I can add a long room on the south, for when the wagons roll again I shall open a trading post."

She turned to Bud, who had come up the slope from the meadow. "You will help Mr. Shafter and learn from him. It is not every man who can build a house."

Ruth Macken had a way of making a man feel large in his tracks, so what could I do but better than my best?

The morning chill spoke of winter coming, yet I notched each log with care and trimmed them with smooth, even blows.

There is a knowledge in the muscles of a workman that goes beyond the mind, a skill that lies in the flesh and the fiber, and my hands and heart held a love for the wood, the good wood whose fresh chips fell cleanly to the left and the right.

Yet as I worked my thoughts worried over the problem of our town. We were ill-prepared for winter, although our sudden decision to stop left us better off than had we pushed on to the westward.

Going on would have been simple, for travel is an escape, and as long as our wagons moved our decisions could be postponed. When one moves, one is locked in the treadmill of travel, and all decisions must await a destination. By choosing to stop we had brought our refuge tumbling about us, and our problems could no longer be avoided.

The promised land is always a distant land, aglow with golden fire. It is a land one never attains, for once attained one faces fulfillment and the knowledge that whatever a land may promise, it may also demand a payment of courage and strength.

To destroy is easy, to build is hard. To scoff is also easy, but to go on in the face of scoffing and to do what is right is the way of a man.

Neely Stuart already regretted the stopping and spoke of continuing on to California in the spring, and Tom Croft, who listened to Neely, was a man who never knew whether the course he had taken was the right one. So he was always open to persuasion. Nor was his Mary of a different mind.

Even Webb talked of going on when spring should again bring grass to the hills, yet he had been the first to break off from the wagon train and follow Ruth Macken in her decision. He was a discontented, irritable man, always impatient for change, yet he was also strong and resolute and would stand up in an emergency. He had a son, an arrogant, disagreeable boy named Foss . . . short for Foster.

John Sampson, my brother Cain, and I were for staying on, which left only Ethan Sackett, a single man who had been guide for the wagon train but had chosen to leave it when we did.

"What has he to do with us?" Webb demanded, when I wondered aloud if Sackett would stay on. "He's a drifter, not one of us."

"He chose to stay with us, and that makes him one of us."

"He chose to stay because of Mrs. Macken. Would he have come with us had it not been for her? I say he does not belong here."

It was our first night around the fire, the first after leaving the wagon train, and we huddled close to the flames for there was an autumn chill in the night. The truth was we were all a little frightened at what we had done, and our nerves were on edge because of it.

"He won't be with us long," Neely Stuart said. "His kind have no stability. He is more like an Indian than a white man."

"Who among us," John Sampson said mildly, "has wintered in this country? I think before the winter is gone we shall be glad he is among us."

"We could have been miles from here," Stuart complained. "We were fools to stop."

"Mrs. Macken," I told them, "will open a store, come spring."

"To sell what?" Stuart scoffed. "And to whom?"

"She will sell boots and clothing she and her husband packed against that purpose and vegetables we ourselves will raise. Whenever possible she will accept goods in payment, goods to be sold again."

"A silly woman's dream!"

"There might be good trade with the wagon trains," Webb admitted, "but no matter. When it is warm again I shall move on."

"I shall stay."

It was the calm voice of my brother, to whom all men listened. Until then he had remained silent, watching the leap of the flames and thinking his thoughts.

Cain's face was square, massive, and might have been hewn from oak. His body was also square, but large and powerful. He moved easily, as one who is in complete command of himself and his every muscle. He was not a man given to talking, speaking only when his mind was made up, not as many men do who shape their thoughts as they speak.

"I shall open my smithy and a shop for the mending of guns. I believe the Widow Macken knows what she is about."

"Stay on if you wish," Stuart said defensively.

"I shall not." Yet his tone had weakened before the weight of my brother's decision.

"I shall leave with the first grass," Tom Croft said. "The wilderness and the thought of Indians distresses my wife."

The sickness of disappointment lay upon me, for if they left our strength would be pared to nothing, and we must also go. We were too few as it was, and if attacked by Indians our chances would be slight.

This valley we had chosen lay upon a highroad for the Shoshone, but it was traveled by the Sioux as well and occasionally by the Ute or Blackfeet. Our presence invited trouble.

On the morning I went up the slope to build for the Widow Macken. There was a fringe of ice along the stream's edge, and the meadow was white with frost. My breath showed in a cloud, and the bodies of the cattle steamed as they worked, hauling down the logs after I felled the trees. . . .

When I had felled my third tree, I put Bud to trimming the limbs, watching him first to be sure he knew the use of an axe, for this was no country in which to be left without a foot. I was beginning the fourth tree when Ethan Sackett rode up the hill to draw rein beside me.

He leaned on the pommel of his saddle and watched for a moment before he spoke. "Bendigo, at this time of year there will be few Indians about, but do you take a walk up the ridge now and again to look over the country. If they are about we must know it, so keep your eyes wide for a sign."

"You believe they are holed up for the winter?"

"Soon . . . but a body can't be too caring. Bendigo, I count on you. I cut little ice with those men down yonder, but neither do I pay it much mind. But if there's trouble comes I figure you'll stand. You and that brother of yours."

"Webb will fight. I have a feeling you can count on him, too. He's a mean, cantankerous man, but come fightin' time, he'll be around."

"You are right, I am thinking. You keep shy of that man, Bendigo. He's dangerous. . . ."

Of a sudden there was a pounding of hoofs, and Ethan turned sharply around, his gun half-drawn under his buckskin shirt.

It was Neely Stuart. He leaned from his horse, trying to peer into the door. "Is Mae here? She went out with the little Shafter girl and Lenny Sampson."

"They were over in the creek bottom when I was cuttin' poles atop the ridge. They should be back by now."

A gust whipped snow into our faces and there was a moan in the wind. For a moment the wind caught our breath and we could not speak.

"Come on!" Neely said. "We'll roust out ever'body and hunt for them."

"You go out there with a lot of tenderfeet," Ethan said, "and you'll lose some of them."

"Who asked you?" Neely shouted. "That's my sister out there!"

Ethan was in no way put out by Neely's anger. "How much experience have you had in blizzards, Stuart? A man can lose himself in fifty yards, and judging by the sound of the wind, this one will be pretty bad."

"Ethan's right," I admitted. "You can't even see the other houses now."

"You coming or not?"

"We're coming," Ethan said. He turned to Ruth Macken. "You'll be all right, ma'am?"

"Bud's here, and we've some unpacking to do and a meal to get. When you come back, come to supper. I'll have some hot soup waiting."

We rode down to town, unable to talk for the wind blowing our words down our throats, yet we thought of what was to come; not one of us was fixed for winter.

It was amazing the way the snow piled up. In the

few minutes it had been falling there were two to three inches on the level, and it was starting to drift against the north side of the cabins.

Neely had reached Cain's house ahead of us, and when we came through the door accompanied by a gust of blown snow he was talking. ". . . if that Sackett opens his mouth in here, I'll . . . !"

"Whatever it is you'll do," Ethan said mildly, "you'd better save it until later. We've got to find those youngsters before they freeze to death."

"You stay out of this!" Stuart shouted. He turned on the others. "Scatter out and hunt for them!"

Ethan squatted on his heels against the wall. "You'd be wanderin' blind in the snow. You start seven men out in a storm like this and some of them aren't comin' back. You've got women-folks will need you before spring comes."

Neely started to shout, but Cain stopped him with a gesture. "What did you have in mind?"

"Bendigo here, he saw those young uns down along the creek, and if they were doin' what I figure, they never saw that storm comin'."

He turned his eyes to Cain Shafter. "I should do the hunting because I know this country better than anybody here, and there ain't anybody going to mind if I don't come back. I'd like Bendigo, if he'd care to come along."

"What about me?" Webb demanded. "I grew up in snow country. I seen a sight of it."

"You're welcome. I spoke of Bendigo because he's single and he's steady. Doesn't fly off the handle. A blizzard in this country is nothing to play around with."

"While you sit here talking those youngsters are freezing!" Neely's voice shook with anger. "Don't you try to tell me what to do! I'm going out!"

"All right. Where do you figure to look?"

"Out there!" Neely flung a wide arm.

"Big country." Ethan got to his feet. "Better take it slow. You get warmed up and you start to sweat. The first time you slow down or stop to rest the sweat will freeze, and you'll be wearing a thin coat of ice next your skin."

"You think they stayed with the creek?" Cain asked.

"Sure. There's hawthorn along the creek, and my guess is they found some late berries hanging. Sometimes they stay on until January, and the first day here I rode down there and saw the bushes heavy with them. Those young uns are hungry for sweet, and it's there, so they probably just went on from bush to bush. When they realized it was snowing heavy they probably stayed right there, knowing we'd come for them."

Ordinarily that would be good thinking, but knowing how flighty Mae Stuart was, I couldn't see her using that much judgment. Mae was sixteen and pretty, but mighty notional. She'd put up her hair about a year back, and she was flouncy, feeling her oats, like. She'd been making eyes at menfolks since she was shy of thirteen and was getting to where she wanted to do something about it.

Ann Shafter, Cain's oldest, was only ten. Lenny Sampson, although a bright youngster, was six ...

The cold was intense. Here or there the snow had heaped itself over a fallen tree or some rocks to form a hollow where an animal or child might have curled up, so we dared pass none of them. Once, slipping on an icy log hidden beneath the snow, I had a bad fall.

When I got up I saw Ethan squatted on his heels, studying something.

It was a rabbit snare, rigged at the opening of a run. The snow around the snare was disturbed and there were flecks of blood, most of them partly covered by snow. Ethan put a finger on the thickest spot of blood, and it smeared slightly under pressure. Almost frozen, but not quite.

"Indians," he said.

We felt a chill beyond that of the cold. Within the hour, no doubt much less than that, an Indian had taken a rabbit from that snare and killed it. He must have been inspecting his snares at the same time that the children were along the creek.

Webb was a hard man, but he had a child of his own, and he knew these children. "Injuns!" he said. "Injuns got them."

The tracks that might have told us more lay under the new fallen snow, and the storm was growing worse. It was only by chance that we had found the snare, for in a few minutes it would have been covered.

We had thought to find the children before they could freeze, perhaps huddled somewhere out of the wind waiting for us . . .

There was nothing to do but go back home. There was a chance they had found their way back, but nobody would have bet on it.

Ethan fell in beside me as we started back. He had faced directly away from that clump of trees, taken the wind at a certain angle on his face, and led off. It was the only guide in a storm like that, and although the wind might shift it wasn't likely to shift that much at this stage of the storm.

"Bendigo, are you game to take a chance? I've a notion where those Indians might be."

"Just the two of us?"

"We'd not make it out and back tonight. Are you with me?"

To my dying day I shall remember that blizzard. Ethan moved up to Cain, who had taken over breaking trail. "Hold across the wind," he advised. "Let it take you on the left eye and nose, like. You'll reach sight of the valley in a few minutes. Once over that low ridge, hold along the edge of the trees above Mrs. Macken's and you'll make it."

Cain stopped. He turned his broad back square to

the wind and looked at Ethan. "What about you?"

"Bendigo an' me, we've an idea. If worst comes to worst we'll just dig a hole in the snow and sit it out. A man can wait out a storm if he doesn't exhaust himself first."

We faced into the storm and plodded away, leaning against the wind. Darkness had come upon us, and the wind blew a full gale, cutting at our exposed brows like knives. It seemed an age before we climbed a knoll and stumbled into a thick stand of aspen where we stopped to catch our breath.

"The day we fetched up to this place," Ethan explained, "I spotted the sign of eight to ten Indians with their travois, lodges, and goods. Not wanting to frighten the women-folks I said nothing. Maybe they were passing through, but that snare was reset, so I figure they're close by."

It was almost still inside the aspen grove. The slim trunks stood so close they formed a barrier against the wind.

"The best place for those Indians to wait out a storm is in the hollow right below this hill, so we're a-goin' down there."

Cold or not, I loosened the buttons on my coat and laid a hand to that old pistol of mine. Never in my born days had I drawn against any man, and I had no mind to unless the need was great.

"You keep that handy. An Indian respects strength but mighty little else."

We went down the hill through the deepening snow, smelling smoke on the wind, and sure enough, the lodges were there, three of them, covered with snow except around the smoke hole at the top where the warmth had melted the snow away.

We listened outside each lodge until we heard Mae speak and some arguing among the Indians. Ethan lifted the flap and went in, with me right behind him.

A small fire burned in the center of the tent, and the air was stifling hot and smoky after the cold outside. Right off I spotted Mae and the youngsters beside her. They seemed unhurt, only scared.

There were five buck Indians in there. One young brave was on his feet arguing, and he was mad as all get-out.

The others were older, and the one at whom the buck seemed to be pointing his words was oldest of all. Now that one might be old, but his eyes were clear, and it seemed to me I saw a gleam of malice in those eyes, like maybe he didn't like that young buck too much.

Talk broke off when we came in, and the young brave put a hand to his tomahawk. The next thing I knew he was looking into the business end of my six-shooter.

Now he was no more surprised than I, for I'd no thought of drawing that gun. It just fetched out when the need came, and young as that warrior was, he knew what that gun meant, and he let go of his tomahawk like it was red hot.

Ethan Sackett, he started talking to that old Indian in Shoshone.

After a minute he stopped talking, and the old man spoke. Ethan interpreted for me out of the side of his mouth. "The young buck wants to keep Mae and kill the young uns, but the old man doesn't like it. He says the Shoshone are friends to the white man.

"He's right about that, but there's more to this argument than a body can see at first glimpse. I think the old man wants to take that young buck down a peg. Gettin' too big for his britches."

My eyes had never left that young warrior. He was mad as a trapped catamount and ready to pitch in and go to fighting.

"Tell them we are friends, Ethan, and tell them to come when the snow leaves and trade with us. Tell them to bring their furs, hides, or whatever.

And thank them for saving the young ones from the snow. Tell them when they come in the spring we will have presents for them."

Sackett, he talked for a while, but before the old man could reply that young buck busted in with a furious harangue, gestering now and again toward the other lodges, like he was about to go for help.

"We'd best take the youngsters and light out," I suggested. "This shapes up to trouble."

Ethan never turned his head. "Mae, get up and come over here and bring the young uns with you."

When the young buck saw what was happening he started to yell, and I belted him in the stomach with my fist. When he doubled over I sledged him across the skull with my gun barrel.

Not one of the others so much as moved, but the old man said something I didn't catch. They didn't seem much upset by what had happened.

Ethan took out his tobacco sack and passed it to the old man, with a gesture implying it was to be shared with the others. Me, I took out my Shafter-made axe, the best there is, and handed it to the old man.

"Friend," I said. Then indicating the axe I said, "It is a medicine axe, made from iron from the skies."

"The youngsters first," Ethan said, "then you."

"I'm holding the gun. You go ahead of me."

We floundered through the snow, which was growing deeper by the moment, and made slow time until we got to the crest of the ridge. My heart was pumping heavily when we topped out, and far off, behind us, we heard shouts.

Ethan led the way, but not toward home. With the youngsters to see to we were in no shape to tackle a trip home through the night and the storm. So Ethan took us into a hollow downwind of the Indians. It was a place gouged out by the fall of two pines whose roots had torn up great masses of earth that clung to a frozen spider web of roots.

When Ethan waded into the hollow he was shoulder-deep, but he floundered around, tramping down the snow. When I saw what he was about, I helped. We tramped down an area five or six feet across, but with snow walls five feet high facing the triangle made by the roots, it was all of eight feet high.

Scooping out a hollow big enough for the kids in one snow wall, I packed the snow tight with my hands.

Ethan found some heavy, broken limbs with which he made a platform for our fire, then he dug under the fallen trees for broken twigs and bark. Soon we had a small fire going, using the mass of earth and roots for a reflector.

We broke off evergreen branches and made a roof across the corner of our hole, and with the falling snow to cover it we soon had a snug snow-house.

We were much too close to the Shoshone camp, and it was a worrisome thing to be without rifles. We had six-shooters, and each of us carried a spare loaded cylinder to be slipped into place if we emptied our guns.

Ann fell asleep in my arms, and Mae put her head on my shoulder, snuggling closer, I thought, than need be. Ethan fixed a bough bed for Lenny Sampson, and he was off to sleep, a mighty tired little boy.

Ethan looked across the fire at me. "We got us a family, Bendigo. Likely the only one I'll ever have."

"You've got no kin?"

He added sticks to the fire. "I've kin-folk a-plenty although I don't recall seeing any of them for years. One was a mountain man like me, a Sackett from the Cumberland River country of Tennessee. Ran into him at a rendezvous on the Green.

"I don't lack for kin-folk. There's Sacketts all over Tennessee and Carolina, but I lack somebody of my very own. When I was shy of fourteen my pa was killed by Comanches on the Sante Fe Trail. Since then I've fetched up and down the country from Missouri to the shores of the western sea, but I hunger for a place of my own and somebody to do for."

Cain's daughter Ann had gone right off to sleep like Lenny, but that Mae was making me nervous, acting like she was asleep but snuggling like she was about to crawl into my lap. If Ethan noticed he paid it no mind.

*Bendigo works hard to help his family, friends and neighbors build the settlement. He has many fast-action adventures in this treacherous wilderness before setting off for the East and a career as a newspaperman.*

*Read the complete Bantam Book, available September 1st, wherever paperbacks are sold.*

# LOUIS L'AMOUR 1

# BANTAM'S #1
## ALL-TIME BESTSELLING AUTHOR
## AMERICA'S FAVORITE WESTERN WRITER

| | | | |
|---|---|---|---|
| ☐ | 13601 | HIGH LONESOME | $1.95 |
| ☐ | 13704 | BORDEN CHANTRY | $1.95 |
| ☐ | 13606 | BRIONNE | $1.95 |
| ☐ | 10618 | THE FERGUSON RIFLE | $1.50 |
| ☐ | 13622 | KILLOE | $1.95 |
| ☐ | 13602 | CONAGHER | $1.95 |
| ☐ | 12862 | NORTH TO THE RAILS | $1.75 |
| ☐ | 12875 | THE MAN FROM SKIBBEREEN | $1.75 |
| ☐ | 12630 | SILVER CANYON | $1.75 |
| ☐ | 12935 | CATLOW | $1.75 |
| ☐ | 12876 | REILLY'S LUCK | $1.75 |
| ☐ | 13611 | GUNS OF THE TIMBERLANDS | $1.95 |
| ☐ | 13605 | HANGING WOMAN CREEK | $1.95 |
| ☐ | 13717 | FALLON | $1.95 |
| ☐ | 10901 | UNDER THE SWEETWATER RIM | $1.50 |
| ☐ | 13152 | MATAGORDA | $1.75 |
| ☐ | 12734 | DARK CANYON | $1.75 |
| ☐ | 12434 | THE CALIFORNIOS | $1.75 |
| ☐ | 12863 | FLINT | $1.75 |

**Buy them at your local bookstore or use this
handy coupon for ordering:**

---

Bantam Books, Inc., Dept. LL1, 414 East Golf Road, Des Plaines, Ill. 60016

Please send me the books I have checked above. I am enclosing $_____
(please add $1.00 to cover postage and handling). Send check or money order
—no cash or C.O.D.'s please.

Mr/Mrs/Miss_____

Address_____

City_____State/Zip_____

LL1—1/80

Please allow four to six weeks for delivery. This offer expires 7/80.